Spotlight

Hanah Gollus

Contents

"Would you want my autograph?"

Emma blinked and frowned. "Why would I want it?" She questioned as she brushed past me with her box of papers. I frowned at her easy dismissal of me.

"You don't want it?" I questioned disbelievingly. Everyone wanted it. Emma turned around and sighed before looking at me with an unimpressed stare. "Yes. I don't. I don't see what I would gain from it. Now, please excuse me. I have work to do."

With that, she continued walking on and I gaped at her, shocked. Did she not like me? Had I offended her in someway? I quickly raced after her and entered a hallway. "I hardly give out autographs you know."

Emma entered a room and I followed. It was most probably her office and she loaded the box onto the table. "You shouldn't be here." She frowned and said as she turned around to face me.

"And I meant it, I don't want your autograph. I'm sorry but I really would like for you to leave." She said firmly as she gestured for me to go.

I opened my mouth and protested. "Did I offend you? Or make you uncomfortable?" I probably sounded pretty desperate but I didn't care. I just wanted to know why this woman was not interested in me.

"Look, uh Jack right? I have nothing against you. I just don't want anything to do with celebrities or Hollywood life okay? And please, you have to leave, you're not authorised to be here and I have loads of work to do."

I nodded and backed away. "Of course. I'm sorry to have kept you away from your work. It was very nice meeting you Emma." I said sincerely and gave one last smile before leaving.

This wasn't the last time she was going to see me. I thought with a grin on my face.

Chapter 1-The Start Of It All

Chapter 1-The Start Of It All

Jack Donnahue's POV

"Karen, you know I love you but, I have to go back home. And, you have to stay here with your family. I have no choice but to leave you." I stared down at the actress, Rachel in front of me hoping that my portrayal of a heartbroken man was coming to pass.

"But Winston, you could stay here. My family accepts you. And what happened to being with me for the rest of our lives?" Rachel gripped onto my arm as her brown eyes pleaded with me.

"I can't. I'm sorry." I said sorrowfully and turned away, waiting for the director to close the scene.

"And cut! Great job guys!" The director yelled and I blew out a breath in relief. I was exhausted and all I needed was a nap and maybe a coffee. An iced coffee. Immediately, I perked at the thought of it.

I had been filming this movie for what seemed like five months already and I had barely gotten much sleep. And I needed it. I had been up till three in the morning filming for one of the scenes and I was beat.

The movie was a cheesy romance film that would be shown when it was almost Valentines Day. Already, I pitied the poor souls whose partners would drag them to watch it. Rachel, the actress playing the female lead grinned at me in acknowledgement and walked off the set to greet her husband and son waiting for her.

Grinning back as a response, I walked off from the set and waited nearby just as one of the interns came towards me. "Jack, the team is taking five. The director said you can come back in an hour or so."

"Thanks." I grinned and the intern walked off. Immediately, I grabbed a cap and some sunglasses before shoving my hands in my pockets and left the building and onto the streets.

I obviously wasn't going to pass off the opportunity to get an iced coffee of my choice because most interns these days just couldn't get my order right.

It could be pretty frustrating when I wanted something that wasn't sweet (considering I wasn't a big fan of sugary sweet stuff) but instead, interns would give me a coffee that tasted like a whole stick of candy floss was added into it.

And well it didn't help when I was a coffee addict who needed my daily cups of iced coffee. (make it at least 3 cups per day).

Looking around, it was clear that my bodyguard, Max had wandered off again. I didn't blame him due to the fact that I had finished filming earlier than expected and obviously Max didn't know.

But hey! I wasn't missing the opportunity to get a coffee now. Walking into a Starbucks chain near the set, I ordered my usual latte and hoped that I was being inconspicuous. But I guess I should've made a better effort in disguising my appearance because a female voice screeched.

"Oh, my god! You're Jack Donnahue! Would you sign my napkin?!" The woman in front of me screeched and shoved the said napkin and a pen towards me. I forced a smile on my face and signed my name quickly before more people could crowd around me.

Oh great. I cursed inwardly and started to panic as more people turned to look at me. Some raised their phones to grab a picture and I quickly shoved some money at the counter and ran out of the shop. Without my coffee.

Running out, I already spotted some reporters and they soon gave chase. Oh, come on! I gritted my teeth as I dashed down the street.

In Hollywood, there were three categories of reporters. One was the paparazzi that wandered around to catch celebrities in compromising situations or just to stalk them. These were the type that were desperate like a pack of vultures on a wounded animal.

Second was the reporters who waited for a scoop to come along and then to report it. They weren't as desperate as the earlier sort I had mentioned earlier and they were my favourite to deal with.

Lastly, was the cool and calm reporters. These were the ones that interviewed you in a talk show or whatnot. Even though they were nice, it was just a front. I swore that behind every fake smile, there was an evil one waiting to pounce the minute anyone slipped up in front of them.

In my opinion, the third category of reporters were the scariest, followed by the first category and then the second. But right now, all I could think of was having a good hiding spot so I could lose the paparazzi on my tail.

I guessed I was too deep in my thoughts that I didn't realise that some of them managed to catch up with me.

"Jack could you give us an interview now?"

"Mr Donnahue, what can you say about the romance between you and supermodel Venice Anderson?"

"Jack! Could you give us an interview about the movie that you're filming now?"

Fuck! I cursed and sprinted off even faster. Right now, I was inwardly thanking any God up there for letting me go to a gym because my stamina for running was way better than these reporters. I continued running and I could hear them chasing me for the rare opportunity where I was without my bodyguard.

I knew I needed a hiding spot soon. No in fact, I needed it right now! Looking around as I ran, I spotted the museum and ran in, hoping to lose them. What I didn't see was the woman holding a box as I crashed into her. And of course, the box fell and papers scattered all over the ground of the almost empty museum.

"Oh great." The woman groaned and I started apologising. "I'm so sorry Miss-"

I cut myself off as the woman ignored me and stood up quickly before starting to stack the papers back into her box. What made me stop was her appearance. Dark silky waves fell slightly pass her shoulders, she had dainty features and pink pouty lips. She had gorgeous hazel eyes and her hair was the colour of dark chocolate.

She was slim and quite tall, around five feet and six inches and she looked about in her mid-twenties. She was wearing a light pink blouse that complimented her pale skin that was paired me with tight black skirt that complimented her long legs. White pointed heels adorned her feet. She was wearing little to no jewelry and her action of picking her papers from the ground stirred me to action.

My brain started functioning and I quickly helped her gather her papers. "I'm really sorry Miss-?" I prompted and the woman gave me the barest of glances and heaved the box onto the counter where the receptionists were no where to be seen.

Well, alright. That reaction was new. I blinked and prompted again. "I'm so sorry Miss- May I have your name so I could properly apologise?" I gave her a charming grin but I could feel my smile falter slightly when her eyes narrowed a little.

"It's Emma." She said after a moment. "Emma? What about a last name?" I grinned and she raised an eyebrow before turning away. "It's just Emma." She said before she started to walk off leaving me gaping at her. Was I actually just dismissed like that?

"Hey! It's just Emma! Do you need help? I can help you carry the box." I called out and teased as I moved to stand in front of her. "No thank you. It's fine. I can manage." She said smoothly and shifted to the left to walk pass me again. Quickly, I side stepped her and started.

"I think I should. After all, I made you drop your paperwork." I flashed her another charming grin and Emma raised an eyebrow before an unimpressed expression took over.

"Yes, it was obvious that you crashed into me. But thank you for your help in picking them up. I really appreciate it. Now please excuse me." She gave a tight smile before quickly walking away.

I could only stare at her retreated form with my jaw on the ground. Was she blatantly ignoring my flirting or was she oblivious to it? All thoughts regarding my annoyance with the reporters was gone and they had been replaced with thoughts about this woman. Emma.

Without thinking, I caught up with her and Emma shot me a frown and questioned. "What are you doing?"

"Would you want my autograph?" I blurted out.

Emma stopped walking and frowned. "Why would I want it?" She questioned as she brushed past me with her box of papers. I frowned at her easy dismissal of me before moving to stand in front of her again. I removed my sunglasses and gave her a grin.

"I'm Jack Donnahue." I stated and waited for Emma to light up and request for my autograph or maybe a photo with her. And maybe she'll pass her number to me. All I received was a blank stare on Emma's pretty face.

"You know, I'm the actor, Jack Donnahue." I prompted and waited for recognition to pass onto her face.

Emma frowned and let out a heavy sigh. "I know that. But I don't want your autograph." She said a little exasperated before walking off again.

"You don't want it?" I questioned disbelievingly. Everyone wanted it. Emma turned around and sighed before looking at me with an unimpressed stare. "Yes. I don't. I don't see what I would gain from it. Now, please excuse me. I have work to do."

With that, she continued walking on and I gaped at her, shocked. Did she not like me? Had I offended her in someway? I quickly raced after her and entered a hallway that looked like it was restricted for staff. "I hardly give out autographs you know." I called out after her. Emma entered a room and I followed. It was most probably her office and she loaded the box onto the table. "You shouldn't be here." She said annoyed as she turned around to face me.

"And I meant it, I don't want your autograph. I'm sorry but I really would like for you to leave." She said firmly as she gestured for me to go.

I opened my mouth and protested. "Did I offend you? Or make you uncomfortable?" I probably sounded pretty desperate but I didn't care. I just wanted to know why this woman was not interested in me or why wasn't she reacting to me like other women would.

"Look, Jack right? I have nothing against you. You had been a perfect gentleman. Except when you entered my office but I just don't want anything to do with celebrities or Hollywood life okay? And I have loads of work to do."

I forced my expression to remain neutral and nodded and backed away. "Of course. I'm sorry to have kept you away from your work. It was very nice meeting you, Emma." I said sincerely and gave one last smile before leaving.

This wasn't the last time she was going to see me. I still had to find out Emma's last name. I quickly slipped on my sunglasses and made sure that my hair was covered by the cap I was wearing.

Looks like the museum would be my next frequently visited place. I thought with a grin on my face as I exited the museum.

* * *

A/N: Hi guys, yes. I decided to start on this right away. I'm so excited to write this book. Let me know what you guys think! If the response is really good, I'll try my best to finish chapter 2 by tomorrow so I can post it!

What do you guys think of Emma and Jack? Let me know in the comments! Love you all!

Chapter 2-The Flowers

Chapter 2-The Flowers

Jack Donnahue's POV

I gave a grin to one of the interns as she handed me my cup of iced coffee. Studying her from the back, her hair was brown but not the exact shade of brown that Emma's hair had. And it didn't look as silky and soft as Emma's-

Frowning a little, I shook my head. Emma had been in my head almost the whole of yesterday. I couldn't decided if her nonchalant attitude towards me was of ignorance or if she was trying to play hard to get.

But seeing that she knew who I was, I came to the conclusion that she was indeed playing hard to get. Which was fine by me seeing that she wasn't the only one who tried that with me. The good thing was that she was interested in me (who wouldn't be?) and that meant I could win her over easily. It also did help that she was gorgeous as hell.

I grinned satisfactorily to myself and my bodyguard Max came towards me. "Hey Max." I greeted and he frowned a little.

"Heard you got into some paparazzi problem yesterday. You should've told me you were leaving the set." He started and I waved my hand dismissively. "It was okay. Not too bad."

"So where were you yesterday? I hoped that you didn't run into any trouble seeing that I wasn't around. And about that, I'm sorry, I didn't know you had finished the scene early." Max questioned as he sipped from his bottle of water.

I flashed him a grin. "I'm fine. Nothing bad happened. Hounded by paparazzi, nothing unusual. I also went to get a coffee."

Max appraised me, "A coffee got you into such a good mood? I doubt it." I gave him a cheeky smile. "Well it did. So, could you uh deliver something for me?" I questioned as Emma's face crossed my mind.

Max raised an eyebrow. "What is it? I'm not going near your sister again if you made her mad. The last time, she almost scratched my eye out."

I grinned sheepishly. "Sorry, but Gwennie can be scary so thanks for being our intermediary. I accidentally stole her cheesecake. I thought it was Strider's!"

Max sighed and shook his head as I mentioned my baby sister and my older brother. "So to who and what?" He questioned with his eyes gleaming with interest and curiosity.

"A woman. A pretty woman." I grinned and Max groaned and covered his face with his hand. "Again? You're such a player Jack."

I shrugged nonchalantly and Max sighed. "Alright what's her name? Where and what?"

"Her name is Emma and she works at the museum near the set and help me get her some flowers. Red roses, jasmines and honeysuckle." I answered and Max got to his feet.

"Okay, Emma what?"

That question stumped me. "That, I don't know. She wouldn't tell me. Just call her 'it's just Emma'. She'll know it." I grinned and instead of the usual look of boredom and exasperation on Max's face, a look of intrigue and amusement appeared.

"You don't know her last name?" Max asked incredulously and I shrugged casually. "Yeah, she didn't want to tell me. But I think she's just playing hard to get you know."

Max blinked before grinning. "Alright then. I'll go get it while you're filming later on. The security on set should be able to handle you." I gave him a grateful smile and punched him in the arm playfully. "Yeah. Thanks. Oh! Make sure she knows its from me."

Max rolled his eyes before ambling off.

* * *

Emmaline Heywood's POV

"So, there was news that someone was after you. And that someone is a certain actor Jack Donnahue." My best friend smirked and I rolled my eyes. Not this again.

"Zachary Richmond. That is quite enough." I said annoyed as I stacked the folders on top of each other while sorting through for a particular folder which was a shipment of Egyptian artefacts from the British museum.

My best friend grinned. "Hey, if you ask me, I think it'll be a match made in heaven. You know seeing your parents are the Heywoods and he's the Jack Donnahue-"

"Could you speak any louder?" I asked irritatedly and glared at Zach. "As far as anyone knows, I'm Emma Greywood. Not Emmaline Grey Heywood. That person disappeared a long time ago. Alright?"

Zach nodded, "I know. I've been with you since then."

My eyes lit up when I saw the file I was looking for. "Good. And you better remember that." I said and Zach grinned at me. "Of course I do. So what did the dashing Jack Donnahue had to say?"

I scoffed before shrugging. "Nothing much. He crashed into me, apologised and left." I answered vaguely and flipped through the folder looking for the dates that the artefacts would be arriving.

Zach let out a low whistle. "Liar. Apparently, Roxanne saw the whole thing. The guy was practically offering to help you with the papers and wanted to know your name."

Damn it! I cursed inwardly. Roxanne was one of the noisiest people I've ever met and the receptionist at the counter in the museum. Figures that when I thought she wasn't around, she was still fishing for gossip.

I gave a flat look to Zach and brushed past him and into my office. My brief meeting with the actor Jack, was nothing really memorable. It was something that I expected from a famous actor who had everyone at his command. And I left that life a long time ago.

Zachary Richmond had been my best friend since I was young and my rock when everything in my life changed about a decade ago.

We had studied in archaeology together and now he was now trying to get a PhD in Archaeology and teaching part time in a university while I worked in a museum. I wasn't aiming to get a PhD like Zachary but I had a B.A for it.

I loved ancient history. It constantly thrilled me knowing that I was holding onto something that wasn't part of the twenty-first century but something from hundreds of years ago.

Glancing at my watch, I exited my office as Zach trailed behind me continuing to tease me about Jack Donnahue. Finally having had enough of it, I turned around and crossed my arms. "Does Gwendolyn really like you and your mouth?"

Zach scowled at me and crossed his arms. "Of course." Finally he remained silent as he shot me a scowl. Satisfied, I continued walking past the receptionist counter to the director's office to hand the folder to him.

On the way, I noticed a tall burly man holding onto a giant bouquet of flowers who was speaking. "I'm here to pass this to a It's Just Emma."

Immediately I stopped and narrowed my eyes. No way did I think what was happening. Behind me, Zach stopped and I turned to him, noticing the amused grin on his face.

And just my luck, Roxanne lit up and grinned. "Oh you mean Emma Greywood?" The man carrying the flowers shrugged. "I think so. I only know her first name."

Roxanne waved her hand dismissively. "Well there's only an Emma Greywood here. So I think that's the Emma you're referring to. Oh! Are those lovely flowers for her?"

The man nodded and grinned. "Yeah. Jack Donnahue sends his best wishes and regards."

I thinned my lips as Roxanne gushed, pleased that she had more gossip to spread. As I walked over to the counter, Roxanne spotted me and beamed. "Emma! Just on time! The actor Jack Donnahue sent these for you!"

The man who delivered the flowers raised an eyebrow and looked at me incredulously. "You're It's just Emma?"

I pursed my lips. "You can say that." The man grinned in amusement and shrugged. "Well Jack sends his regards to you and those flowers are for you." He gestured to the large bouquet of flowers on the counter.

Behind me Zach was snickering away and I shot him a harsh glare. Turning back to the man, I shook my head and shot him a polite smile. "Thank you for them but I'm sorry. Please, do send them back to Mr. Donnahue."

The man blinked in surprise. "But he insists it is for you Miss Greywood."

Zach burst into laughter and I nudged him in the gut with my elbow. Noticing that the man had found out the surname I had taken, I pursed my lips in slight irritation. "Like I said, please do send them back, I don't have a particular fancy for flowers." I stated firmly and the man grinned in amusement.

"If you say so Miss. Good day." He nodded his head and took the flowers and walked off.

I blew out a breath and waited for the wolves to pounce. Three, two, one...

"Oh Emma! How exciting! Jack Donnahue likes you!" Roxanne gushed. "Hardly." I murmured and Roxanne frowned. "Why not? He's hot! You can't deny that! He even sent you flowers which you rejected and I can't believe you did that!"

I plastered on a tight smile and clutched the folder tightly. "I don't see anything special about him. Excuse me Roxanne." I gave her a nod and a polite smile before hurrying off.

"Oh come on Emma! You got to admit that this is interesting as hell!" Zach called out after me. Waiting for him to catch up with me so I could speak, I scowled at him.

"Hardly. I don't have time to be an actor's plaything. I have responsibilities such as Ella. She's only five years old and her dad is in hospital while her mother couldn't care less about her while she's jetting off around the world."

Zach sighed and turned serious. "You're right. But Ella is going to be fine. She has you and you're the best aunt anyone can ask for."

I bit my lip at that. "Thank you. I just want Theo to wake up so badly." I choked up a little at that. It was hard to see my twin in a coma.

Without any words, Zach pulled me into a hug and I shut my eyes and leaned into his embrace. Pulling away, I offered him a small smile. "Thank you. And seeing that you were being so nice today, I won't tell your fiancée that you thought she was bitchy as hell when you first met her."

Zach scoffed and crossed his arms, his bright blue eyes were filled with amusement. "I dare you to do so and I'll personally go over to Jack Donnahue and tell him you like him.

"Yeah right. You wouldn't dare." I warned and Zach shrugged. "Why not? I would. I have the guts." He grinned at me and I rolled my eyes. "Alright. Seeing that you're here to drop me off because my car is in repairs, wait here while I pass the folder to the director." I instructed and Zach shrugged and shoved his hands into his pockets.

Quickly passing the files to the director, I hurried out and left with Zachary to get Ella from kindergarten as her babysitter was sick today. Zach drove and we sat in comfortable silence. But knowing Zach, he was surely unable to remain silent for too long.

"So..." He started before trailing off.

I suppressed a smile. Knew it. "Yes?" I questioned and Zach glanced at me before turning his attention back to the road. "I'm just worried about you Em."

I chewed on my lower lip. "I'm fine. I've got you, Ella and my beloved job. I'm alright."

Zach sighed heavily. "I know that. But you need to loosen up. And with Ella and whatnot, you've not living to the fullest you know."

"I'm fine Zach. I don't have that luxury in my life. Not anymore." I said with finality lacing my words and thankfully Zach dropped the subject.

Sighing inwardly, I just wished that the flowers that Jack Donnahue had sent would be the last I would hear from him.

* * *

A/N: Hi! Overwhelmed by the amazing responses from the previous chapter! You guys are amazing! And I'm really glad you like Jack's character. This is an insight to how Emma thinks and her feelings and thoughts.

I am really pleased about the comments and whatnot. Please show this baby some love too so vote and comment to let me know what you guys think about Emma and Jack! <3 I think this is the first book to be written by me that displays gifs for both the hero and heroine. Ahaha. Hope you guys love this chapter and thank you so much for reading! <3

Chapter 3-The Rejection

Chapter 3-The Rejection

Jack Donnahue's POV

"What do you mean you brought the flowers back?" I frowned.

"She didn't want it and the florists do not accept refunds or returns." Max repeated and shoved the flowers into my hands. "Well did you say it was from me?" I pressed and Max grinned. "Yeah. She says she doesn't like flowers."

I blinked and burst into laughter. "What are you saying? Everyone likes flowers. How can she not like flowers?"

Max rolled his eyes and took the flowers away from my grasp and set it down onto the table beside us. "That's what I'm saying. I believe her exact words were: I don't have a particular fancy for flowers."

That did sound like what Emma would have said (even though I only met her for like ten minutes). "You're kidding." All traces of amusement and laughter was gone from my face. "But everyone loves flowers!" I protested.

Max shrugged and shoved his hands into his pockets. "Well, not her." I frowned. "Well, what did she say when she realised that it was from me?" I asked hopefully.

Max grinned knowingly. "She wasn't really pleased. In fact she looked quite annoyed to see me and the flowers."

"Oh." I clenched my jaw and my face fell while my mind was already thinking of ways to win her over. But seriously, wasn't flowers something everyone liked? And wasn't it considered romantic or something? Or had I learned it all wrong from my sister and my sister-in-laws?

"But Jack, I have to ask why exactly are you interested in her? She seems to not even like you and she's not really your type." Max questioned with a grin as he studied me.

I scoffed and scrolled through the web on my phone, looking for the number of the museum. "What are you talking about? Everyone is my type."

Max rolled his eyes before listing off, "She's smart, she's pretty and she has head screwed on tight. Not like those other women you hung out with."

"Hey! Natalie was smart alright!" I said defensively.

"Yeah I thought so too until she claimed that Mt. Everest was a volcano." Max commented dryly and I frowned, "Yeah, well what about Kayla?"

"She thought Hollywood was a state here in the U.S."

I stifled a grin at the absurdity of some of the flings I had in the past but seeing the look of absolute disbelief on Max's face as he recalled all those past experiences, I couldn't help but let my mouth twitch before bursting into laughter.

"Yeah, go ahead and laugh. But all I can say is, this woman you're after, she's too smart for you."

Looking up at him, "What do you mean by that?" I questioned as I studied the flowers on the table. Max sighed and sat opposite me.

"She's way out of your league. She works in a museum and she looks very smart. And from what I saw yesterday, she might have a boyfriend."

I frowned at that, "How can she be out of my league? I'm Jack Donnahue, an A-list actor!"

Max rolled his eyes and crossed his arms. "Yeah, all you have to do is recite a couple of lines in front of a camera and look pretty-"

"Hey!" I retorted defensively and Max ignored me and continued. "Well, like I said earlier, Emma Greywood is way smarter than you."

I perked up upon hearing that. "Her last name is Greywood?" Max nodded his head. "Yes, though once again, she didn't seem too pleased to know that I knew her surname."

I grinned at that. Emma Greywood. Crap, her name sounded even better than 'It's Just Emma'. Now, I was contemplating what was my next move. She didn't like flowers, she didn't seem to like me. Time to pay her a little visit because hearing about her reactions was one thing, but seeing them for myself was another.

And it must be fate considering that the shooting for my next scene would be fours hours from now. I had loads of time to get a coffee and to ask Emma out.

"Max, let's go get a coffee, after, we'll be visiting the museum." I grinned in anticipation as I got to my feet.

"Oh Jack." He sighed heavily and pinched the bridge of his nose in exasperation.

* * *

I entered the museum once again, but this time, I didn't have my cap or sunglasses seeing that Max was trailing behind me, looking for any suspicious people. Also known as the paparazzi.

I knew some stares were thrown my way and whispers among the visitors of the museum could be heard. Heading to the receptionist counter, I flashed a friendly smile to the receptionist and opened my mouth to speak.

But before I could, she started. "Oh my god you're Jack Donnahue!" She gushed excitedly and I grinned. "Yeah. Hi, would you mind telling me where Emma Greywood is?"

The receptionist who was in her late fifties almost swooned and she gasped in excitement. Her chest was heaving from her heavy breathing as she gasped excitedly and for a brief moment, I feared that she would faint and hope that I would give her CPR. Quickly, I flashed her a bright grin and she brightened up.

"Of course. I heard about the whole thing with Emma. She's quite the catch isn't she? But she's really difficult but like I always tell my sons, the way to a girl's heart is to be her Prince Charming! And oh! I loved that movie you did about you being undercover spy in that country! You were amazing!" She gushed and I shrugged bashfully.

"Thank you, but it was all thanks to the writer of that story and all the crew members and the director." I said awkwardly and if it was even possible, the receptionist gasped once more.

God, I really hoped that she wouldn't expect me to give her CPR if she fainted. I shuddered and shoved my hands in my pockets. "So may I see Emma?"

The receptionist bobbed her head excitedly before picking up the phone. I waited and gave a hesitant grin to the people around me and Max stepped nearer to me as more people began noticing me.

And I guessed that Max was pretty intimidating. He was well built and pretty tall with his sunglasses. Right now, he had his face set into a permanent scowl.

"Alright! Emma would be right down, but I didn't tell her you came to see her. If not she wouldn't even come down." The receptionist known as Roxanne beamed and focused her attention on me.

"So Mr. Donnahue, or may I call you Jack?" She started and I grinned, "Jack is fine-"

"Great! So I heard the movie you're filming now is almost finished!"

I nodded, "Yeah, it's coming out two days before Valentine's Day."

Roxanne nodded and her eyes lit up and she called out, "Emma! Look who's here for you!"

Immediately, I turned around and the sight of Emma Greywood almost made me lose the composure I had. Her wavy brown hair was let down and she had a black dress on with a white jacket and silver flats.

However, the frown on her face made my chest sink a little. Oh god, she did not look pleased. Not one bit. I was not going to give up, Emma intrigued me and I quickly pasted on a charming grin.

At that, her frown seemed to deepen and her eyes narrowed to Roxanne with an accusing stare. Behind me, I could hear Max chuckling to himself.

Emma walked towards us and stopped a metre away from us. "Roxanne, you said there was something important?" She questioned a little frostily and Roxanne nodded and gushed excitedly. "Yes, Jack Donnahue is here to see you!"

Emma's brown eyes flickered to mine and she thinned her lips before replying casually, "I would hardly classify that as something important."

My jaw dropped.

Wasn't I important enough? Behind me, Max was stifling his laughter and I forced a smile on my face. Roxanne gasped at Emma's response and she continued. "But he wants to see you!"

Emma studied me and raised an eyebrow. "Hi, how may I help you?" She questioned emotionlessly and I forced myself to talk. "I wanted to talk to you."

Emma blinked and behind me, Max coughed and mumbled under his breath. "Smooth Donnahue."

I turned back and glared at him. He was certainly not helping! Emma opened her mouth to respond when she noticed the various eyes on us. Straightening, she nodded reluctantly and gestured for Max and I to follow after her.

Was she changing her mind about me? I thought hopefully and greeted Roxanne goodbye before following after Emma. My eyes slid down her slim figure, noticing the way her dress clung to her curves and how her wavy brown hair seemed lighter under the lights.

She entered her office before turning to me. "What do you want?" She questioned and her eyes narrowed at Max but turned her attention towards me.

"A date." I blurted out.

Jesus Jack! You're losing your cool around this woman! I cursed inwardly. Once again, Emma didn't react like how I expected most women would. She didn't brighten up excitedly and say yes.

Instead, her frown grew even colder and she glanced away before meeting my earnest gaze straight on. "I'm sorry but I would have to decline."

I frowned, was she still playing hard to get? She already had my attention! Why was she still resisting? "Why not?" I questioned.

Emma crossed her arms and for just a few seconds, I was so tempted not to observe that her breasts was pushed up by her arms. "I'm sorry but no thank you. I'm very busy and I don't have the time to date anyone. Especially you." She said calmly.

Frowning, I mimicked her and crossed my arms and questioned defensively. "What do you mean by that?"

By the unimpressed gaze that she was giving me, I knew Emma was not pleased. "I meant whatever you're feeling offended about." She replied distantly and walked behind her desk.

"What's wrong with me?" I questioned a little annoyed. Emma Greywood hardly knew me, who was she to judge me just on ten minutes of talking to me?

"Tell me honestly. Are you someone who thinks that every woman would kill to go out with you? Do you think that the world revolves around you? That you're one of the most important and special people in the world? Would you do anything-absolutely anything to remain where you are in the world today?" Emma questioned defiantly, her eyes were bright as she studied me.

Her questions stumped me and Max inhaled sharply, his gaze darting between Emma and I. Her questions were hitting a little too close to home. Well, not all of them, but at least one.

Pulling myself together, I flashed her another grin and replied. "Uhm, yes, no, no, no."

Emma cocked an eyebrow. "You don't think you're one of the most important and special people in the world?" She questioned disbelievingly.

I grinned and shrugged. "No, there's other people way more important and special than me. Like my family?"

The sight of Emma's lips twitching as she fought to smile made me pump my fist in the air inwardly. I was finally gaining some ground with her!

Emma quickly composed herself and straightened. "Jack, I'm really sorry but, I would still have to say no. I don't want to get involved with people from Hollywood-"

"Technically, I'm from Boston." I interrupted and Emma rolled her eyes while shooting me a flat look. "You know what I mean. Anyway, like I said earlier, I don't have time to date. I have my job and responsibilities."

"You seem like you're in your twenties, what kind of responsibilities do you have?" I questioned, wanting to know more about the enigma that was Emma Greywood.

Emma narrowed her eyes at me and said coolly. "Important ones."

Immediately, I knew it was time to back away. I had tried scaling her walls and I almost passed one of them but she piled them higher than before.

And right now, I knew that I wouldn't be able to know about her even more seeing that she was on the defence. Like any good general in a war, I knew when it was time to strike and when to retreat.

Looking at the wary expression on Emma's face, I decided to retreat. I nodded my head. I wasn't admitting defeat and neither was I pursuing her actively now. I was just going to leave her into a false sense of security before striking.

"Alright then, I guess, I'll see you soon Emma." I offered and Emma scrutinised me suspiciously before giving a small nod.

"I hope not. It was nice meeting you Jack, but I hope I do not have to see you again. I don't want your world to get into mine." She stated before turning away, dismissing me like I was nothing. Or like a boss getting rid of one of her employees.

The image of her in a tight black skirt and a white blouse flashed into my mind and I had to shake some sense into myself. Jesus, I was being ridiculous!

I quickly left her office, not wanting her to have her annoyed at me and Max quickly trailed after me. Without looking at him, I muttered. "Not one word Max."

Immediately, Max burst into laughter and ignored my warning. "Oh god! I've never seen anyone, not even your family shut you down like that!"

Ignoring him as we left the museum, my mind was filled with thoughts about her. Emma Greywood. A sneaky grin slipped onto my face while I mentally rubbed my hands together in anticipation.

I never backed down from a challenge. Especially if it was from a woman I was interested in.

* * *

A/N: Hey guys! Here is the next chapter! And I hope you guys love it. Please leave a comment and vote! It'll mean so much to me and it'll be really cool to hit 10k reads and 1k votes!

Let me know your thoughts on this, what do you think on both Jack and Emma. I really love hearing your thoughts on opinions! So let me know! Also, thanks so much for reading and I love you all! <3 <3

Chapter 4-The Chase

Chapter 4-The Chase

Emmaline Heywood's POV

"Aunt Emma!" My niece yelled. I frowned and stopped walking before I could get into the car.

"What is it Ella? Did you forget something?" I questioned as I bent down to be almost the same height as my blonde haired niece.

Ella shook her head. "No. But can we have pasta for dinner?" She begged, her big brown eyes pleading and my breath hitched as those very brown eyes were the exact kind that my brother had. Theo's eyes were a darker shade of brown unlike my lighter hazel brown eyes.

Pushing back the sudden burst of emotion that swelled up in me, I smiled and nodded. "Of course. And to make it better, I'll get ice-cream!"

Ella brightened and she nodded her head eagerly. "Yes please!"

I beamed and kissed her forehead and watched as she ran back towards her teacher that was waiting for her. Very few people knew that Ella was the daughter of Theo Heywood, the man that was in a coma due to a drug overdose and also my twin.

I pressed my lips tightly at that and turned back to my car. Theo had been in a coma for about ten months now and if he reached the duration of a year, the chances of him waking up was slim to none.

I got into my car and just stared at the road in front of me. I was thankful that I had not started driving yet and therefore, no one would be sounding their car horns at me for not moving.

I breathed deeply, trying to compose myself and once I felt that my emotions were under control, I started driving. Seeing that it was a Friday, I didn't have to go for work. I only worked four days a week at the museum while Friday, I worked from home.

And I was so thankful to have Bethany, Ella's babysitter to pick Ella from kindergarten everyday and to watch over her until I came back from work.

I knew raising a five year old wasn't easy but hell, I hated Ella's mother for abandoning her just so that she could jet around the world as a supermodel. Ella had only came to my care when Theo had been in a coma for a month.

That meant that he still didn't know that he was a dad. I didn't demand for a paternity test to be taken. Ella looked exactly like her father with the exception of her blonde locks which she had gotten from her mother.

But I was also thankful that no one knew that actor Theo Heywood and supermodel Willa George had a child. Ella didn't deserve to be in the toxic world that was Hollywood. She needed a regular home with love and care and I just hoped that I was enough for her.

Glancing at my watch, I realised that I had some time to grab some groceries before the part time cleaner I had hired to clean my house was to arrive.

Driving to the supermarket and after parking my car. I almost choked at the sight of Jack Donnahue advertising for some sort of shampoo that was displayed on the windows.

Why was it after our brief meeting that I was beginning to notice where he was appearing. Be it newspapers, advertisements and on television. It was quite disconcerting to be honest.

My impression on him had been spot on and I didn't care for his attitude. He was exactly what Hollywood was and I didn't want anything to do with it.

Grabbing a trolley, I looked through the aisle and checked through my mental list of items that I needed to get.

Looking through the various selection of frozen pizza in the frozen department. Sighing, I quickly tossed two boxes of pepperoni into my shopping basket for those days that I was too lazy to cook.

Heading towards the section where they sold ice-cream, I searched through the cartons for Ella's favourite flavour, Raspberry.

My eyes scanned through the different assortments of ice-cream. Chocolate, mint, vanilla, cookies and cream, butterscotch. My eyes lit up at that. While Ella's favourite flavour was raspberry, mine was butterscotch and god, did I love it.

Placing the carton in the trolley, I scanned through the shelves searching for a raspberry flavoured ice-cream so that Ella and I could watch some Disney movies together.

"What are you looking for?"

I almost jumped from shock and whirled around to see Jack Donnahue in person (not from the advertisement) as he grinned at me.

I almost wanted to laugh at how ridiculous he looked with a blonde wig on his head followed by a cap and another pair of sunglasses. But what made me almost lose it was the fake beard on his jaw.

"What are you doing here? Where's your bodyguard?" I questioned, a little annoyed that he had not stayed away from me like I hoped.

Jack grinned and took his sunglasses off. "Oh I told Max I would be fine while I just grabbed some pre-made coffee from the drinks section and I saw you standing here glaring at the innocent ice-cream."

I rolled my eyes at that. "Why the wig and the beard? The last time, you didn't bother with those."

He grinned and I eyed him warily. "Oh this disguise is to help me blend in from fans and crazy stalkers and the paparazzi since Max isn't here."

I stiffened. Oh god, how could I have forgotten that paparazzi constantly followed famous actors like Jack Donnahue around. There was no way that I wanted my face to be captured with his! I couldn't! I had Ella to think about now.

I stepped away from him and noticed the small frown that formed on his face and quickly faced the front. From the corner of my eye, I noticed the carton with an image of raspberries on it and my eyes lit up.

Taking it from the fridge, I placed it in my trolley and walked off, hoping that Jack wouldn't follow me. But of course, luck was never with me because that was exactly what Jack did.

"Hey! Emma, where are you going?" He called after me and caught up with me.

"Please go away. I'm busy." I ordered as I quickened my pace away from him. Seriously, what does it take to get rid of someone? It wasn't that hard for him to take a hint was it?

"But I want to talk to you." Jack called as he trailed behind with a charming grin on his face. I scowled and shot him an annoyed glance. "Well too bad we can't always get what we want in life."

At my response, Jack burst into laughter and I couldn't help but smile a little that I had made the Jack Donnahue laugh.

I quickly pushed the trolley into the next aisle and froze when I was met with rows of boxes of condoms and pregnancy tests.

Oh god.

I cursed inwardly and behind me, I could hear Jack snickering under his breath but that stopped when I gave him a harsh glare.

Quickly moving on to the next aisle and picked up a carton of apple juice for Ella and some cereal. Jack walked beside me and shoved his hands into his pockets.

Feeling a little unnerved from the Jack's attention on me as I did my grocery shopping, I stopped moving and turned to Jack and frowned. "Don't you have to go now?"

Jack blinked and I almost broke into a smile again from how silly he looked but I restrained myself. "Yeah, but I'm not in a rush. I can hang around with you."

I frowned at that and studied him. "Why? If you're doing all of this just to get a date with me, sorry, you're going to be disappointed."

"But why not? I'm funny and you're funny. It'll be fun!"

What was he, twelve? "I'm funny?" I questioned dryly and Jack grinned. "Yeah. You're hilarious. So why not, go out with me for dinner."

I raised an eyebrow before stating. "No." With that, I turned around and began searching for the pasta sauce that Ella liked.

"Well, give me ten reasons why not." He requested and I continued scanning the shelves for the jar and answered without even sparing him a single glance.

"Just because. No. Not interested. Busy. Don't have the time. Work. Responsibilities. I don't like you. Can't be bothered and again, no." I replied nonchalantly, hoping that he would be offended and give up.

Jack snickered and I groaned. Why wasn't he going away? "Emma, busy and not having the time is the same thing. Also you replied no twice. So I'll see you tomorrow!"

I whirled around and scowled at him. "Can't you take a hint? I'm not interested. I'm sure that there are other women who would love to have this opportunity with you. But I don't."

Jack frowned and followed after me silently as I continued to look for shredded cheese. Turning to look at him before commenting dryly. "I'm surprised that you're not out of here already. Most men wouldn't be able to take so much blows to their ego."

He shrugged, and my eyes discreetly noticed the way his biceps flexed before moving back to his face. "Yeah, but, I'm not most men. I'm Jack Donnahue."

I rolled my eyes at his comment. He really did have an abnormally huge ego. "And I'll have you know that there's more to me than a pretty face."

Raising my eyebrows, I eyed him skeptically, "What else do you have besides a pretty face?"

Jack blinked and a bright grin curved his face. "You think I have a pretty face?"

I shot him a dry look. "Most actors and actresses must have a pretty face. You're not that special." Jack's bright grin fell and I almost felt bad but I quickly turned away.

"Well, like I have yet to say, I really am more than just a pretty face. I went to college." He offered and I raised an eyebrow. "So?"

Jack seemed lost for words at my response and he quickly replied. "Well, I have an education."

"Like almost everyone else." I rebuffed and turned to the next aisle to look for Ella's favourite candy. From the corner of my eye, I noticed Jack slapping his cheek and muttering under his breath.

Guilt hit me, I knew I was being harsh and I sighed before stopping abruptly. Behind me Jack almost crashed into me but stopped himself just in time.

"Jack, look. You've been very nice and a perfect gentleman, but I'm not going out with you. I'm sorry." I said politely and Jack frowned.

"Why not if I had been a perfect gentleman?" He protested and quickly shoved his sunglasses back on when a couple of teenage girls walked passed us discussing actors and actresses.

I lifted an eyebrow at that. "That. I don't want to be famous or known as one of your women. I want to live my life as privately as possible."

"I can make sure you'll stay out of the spotlight. My bodyguard Max has friends-" He started and I pressed my lips into a thin line and cut him off.

"Tell me honestly, you only asked me out because I turned you down right?"

To my satisfaction, Jack's jaw worked for a moment to come up with a reply and eventually he remained silent and I gave him a small knowing smile. "It's fine. But I hope that you'll leave me alone from now. I really don't want to go out on a date with you."

"Jack!" I turned around to see Jack's bodyguard walking towards us with a concerned look on his face that faded as recognition took over when he spotted me.

"Miss Greywood, it's nice to see you." He greeted and I offered him a smile. "Hi, you must be Max."

He smiled at me before turning to Jack, "Gabriel, we need to go now. Get your coffee quickly."

I frowned. Who was Gabriel? "Gabriel's my first name." Jack offered seeing the confusion on my face.

"Oh." I murmured as I pronounced his full name in my head. Gabriel Jack Donnahue. Why the heck was his name that sexy?

"Jack hurry! The paparazzi is here!" Max called urgently and my eyes widened in alarm. I could not be seen with Jack Donnahue. Moving away, i greeted Max and Jack goodbye while trying to leave as much distance as I could from Jack and I didn't give him a backward glance.

Later that night, Ella and I sat on the couch as Cinderella was playing, ice-cream cartons in our hands as we ate and watched simultaneously.

Watching Cinderella find true love with her Prince almost made me sigh wistfully. If only life was that easy and beautiful.

It certainly wasn't. I had the scars to prove that. Looking down at Ella with ice-cream all over her mouth as she watched the film with rapt attention, I couldn't help but smile.

With Ella, I was contented with my life the way it is, I didn't need Prince Charming to sweep me off my feet. Life was fine the way it was.

* * *

A/N: Hi guys! Here is the next update! I hope you all liked it! Please vote and comment to let me know what you guys think! Thanks so much for reading and I hope you like it! <3

P.S. Could you guys recommend any fantastic Dramione fanfics with smut scenes? Lmao.

Chapter 5-The Donnahue Family

- -

Chapter 5-The Donnahue Family

Jack Donnahue's POV

How the hell, was Emma Greywood so spot on about me?

How the hell did she know things or realise certain things about me that I didn't even know yet. After I did some reflecting, I realised I only wanted her to go out with me because she refused. And that she was gorgeous.

And her pointing that out made me feel like a major dick. No wonder she didn't want anything to do with me. My mother would be swimming laps in her grave right now if she knew what I had turned into.

I knew I had to apologise. But what if Emma thought that I only apologised so that she would go out with me? I couldn't have that. If I ever apologised, I would mean it.

One thing for sure, I was not going to hunt her down at the museum later on, not today definitely. My ego had taken too many hits and I wasn't sure if I could take anymore before losing my cool.

But strangely, while she shot those quick witted remarks at me, I wasn't pissed at her. But more at myself for not knowing what to say. The entire time at the grocery store, I had been wondering what to say to her as she knocked my ego down blow by blow.

To be very very honest with myself, I was impressed with Emma's response. Not only did she manage to make me a stumbling fool but her remarks were sharp and witty and yet classy. And I actually prided myself being the King of witty remarks but I guess I had to renounce that title and hand it over to Emma.

Never had I been turned down in that sort of manner before, until Emma. Sure, some women rejected me but they never made me want to chase after them even though they said no.

What was it about Emma Greywood?

Max had left after driving me home and I entered my house to see my nephews and niece running about. God, fuck no, I really did not want to deal with them now. The appearance of my nephews and niece meant that-

"Jack! Hurry up!" My sister hollered and I entered my living room to see all of my siblings waiting for me.

"Okay, this has got to stop! I mean seriously this is my house! How on earth did you even manage to enter without keys?" I demanded as I spotted all four of my siblings and with their respective partners (except for Gwennie and Emmett)

My oldest brother, Cameron shrugged while his wife, Daniella answered. "Your bodyguards let us in." While at the same time, my second oldest brother's wife, Isadora answered. "I picked the lock."

"Well, not that I'm not happy to see you. Why are you guys here?" I questioned and my sister, Gwennie glared at me condescendingly. "I have news to tell everybody." She announced and gestured for me to sit.

"Alright. But why my house?" I questioned a little annoyed.

"Because your house is bigger than mine. Well, until I get married. And that's what I have to say. I'm engaged. Zach proposed just the other day." Gwen announced brightly as she flaunted the diamond ring on her hand.

Immediately, all of us stood up and congratulated her. Jesus, even my younger sister was attached, I groaned inwardly. My two older brothers were married and now Gwennie was engaged. At least my youngest brother, Emmett was still single.

I crossed my arms. "Gwennie, why isn't Zach here with you? All of you have met him once while I have not." I pointed out with a frown. "And isn't it a little odd that you're announcing this on your own? How scandalous." I smirked.

Gwen snorted and crossed her arms. "I didn't tell him that I was going to tell all of you. You guys are insane and you're going to ruin it if he was here. And it's too bad for you that you were filming in Alaska back then."

Isadora scoffed and tossed her hair over her shoulder. "Right. Bullshit."

Ugh, oh god no. Here it was. I immediately slumped onto the sofa and shut my eyes, waiting for it to start.

"What's that supposed to mean?" Gwen demanded and Isadora retorted. "Just admit that you're as insane as all of us are."

"Strider put a leash on your wife!" Gwen yelled and Strider stepped in. "Isa, not now. You're pregnant, don't get stressed up. Gwen, stop goading her."

I watched the scene with mild interest, while wondering who was going to win. My two nephews and niece burst into the room yelling about a giant fly and went to their respective parents.

Daniella sighed before crossing her arms as her son and daughter, Logan and Lia (who were twins) crowded around her. My other nephew, Phillip went to Isadora who was still arguing with Gwen while Strider tried to put out the flames that was my sister and my sister-in-law.

My younger brother Emmett sat beside me, his eyes fixed on watching our siblings argue and fight. This was actually a normal occurrence in the Donnahue family.

"Emmett, make sure you don't get attached to women like that alright? Also, not the smart ones because then, they can knock you on your ass like mine got handed to me today." I mumbled under my breath.

And of course, amidst all the shouting and arguing, I could still be heard. Typical. Gwennie frowned. "What did you say?"

My older brothers watched me with surprise in their eyes and Daniella and Isadora stared at me with interest. Ah fuck. Should have kept my mouth shut.

"Which woman handed your ass to you?" Isadora demanded as interest lighted up in her green eyes. Gwennie glared at me. "Why am I just hearing about this now? Jack!"

Someone shoot me already.

"What woman?" Gwennie demanded and I groaned and banged my head against the head rest of my sofa. "She's no one alright! Mind your own business!" I glared and Gwennie scoffed.

"Yeah right! What woman? Gabriel Jack Donnahue! If you don't spill your guts, I'm coming after you!" Gwennie demanded as my sister-in-laws crowded around me poking and prodding for details.

I glared at my older brothers who looked away, letting their wives and my sister continuing to demand and question me. Jesus, what the hell. Since when was the Donnahue family run by women when I thought we were all equals?

* * *

I sipped from my can of beer as my siblings messed about in my kitchen. As usual, Daniella and Cameron were cooking while Gwennie was watching over the children and both Emmett and Strider was discussing about politics.

How utterly boring.

I was left alone and sat in the corner of my living room sipping from my can of beer. But of course, I should've known that no disturbances from my family members meant that something was up.

Just as this thought came into my mind, Isadora sidled up to me with a can of coke which I was sure that my brother had forced her to drink instead of a cup of coffee.

"Jack... So who's the lady? Don't worry. No one else is listening." She grinned slyly and I rolled my eyes. "Yeah, right, like I'm telling you. I'm sure that they all put you up to it."

Isadora scoffed and crossed her arms as she coaxed. "Come on Jack, I could try to help give you a woman's perspective on things." She smirked smugly, as if she thought that would let me spill everything to her.

Sadly she was right. There was no way I was confiding in Gwennie. She would ruin things between Emma and I (or make things worse because there wasn't anything going on in the first place). And I really wanted a female perspective on what the hell was going on in Emma's mind.

I couldn't tell Daniella, she was too perceptive on things and she would definitely tell Cameron who in turn would tell Strider and who in turn would tell Isadora. And of course, Isadora would brag about knowing it to Gwennie who would complain about it to Emmett and me.

Well at least, I knew Isadora would keep it quiet if she knew how serious I was. She may be a lot of things-brash and demanding, but she was loyal to a fault.

"I'm serious. If word gets out, I'll tell Strider about the anniversary present you got him." I warned and Isadora narrowed her eyes. "Fine. So who exactly is this woman who handed your ass to you?"

I grinned as the thought of Emma Greywood came to mind. "She's smart, really smart and well, she won't go out with me."

Isadora scoffed, "Obviously, since I believe no smart woman would go out with you."

I shot her a flat look and she burst into laughter. "Alright, alright. I'll be serious now. What's her name?" She studied me and I shrugged. "I'm not telling you that. You'll hunt her down."

My sister-in-law pursed her lips, clearly not denying that and frowned. "So did she say why she doesn't want to go out with you?" Isadora probed and I shrugged.

"She doesn't want anything to do with my lifestyle. Like she has no interest in Hollywood." I answered unhelpfully and Isadora shrugged. "Then you should leave her alone and respect her wishes."

I groaned. "No shit. It doesn't take a genius to know that!"

Isadora shrugged unrepentantly before commenting. "Well, I said I could try to give you some help but she clearly wants nothing to do with you. That's pretty obvious. What's so special about her anyway?"

"I don't know," I stated and Isadora sighed. "Well, I hope you would get over this. And I have to go. Your nephew is kicking my fucking bladder." She cursed and walked off in her flats, not the usual high heels she was wont to wear.

Sometimes, I did wonder how the hell did my reserved formal brother who was a stickler for propriety ever married a woman who was the total opposite of him.

Strider was someone who was formal with everyone, reserved with strangers or well everyone except his family. While Isadora on the other hand, was someone who was brash, demanding, rude, obnoxious at times, and vulgar.

It totally baffled my mind. Their son Phillip was about three years old and now, Isadora is pregnant with their second child.

Cameron, my oldest brother was someone who I wasn't particularly close to considering we were total opposites. While his wife, Daniella was fun and humorous which was everything that Cameron wasn't. They had twins, Logan and Lia who were about five years old.

I was literally the middle child while Gwennie was born after me. Even though she was the only girl in the family, she was still quite a tomboy. However, I had to say that she was spoilt and demanding as hell too. That was most probably why she couldn't always get along with Isadora as their personalities were almost alike.

Emmett, the youngest in our family of five, was shy, quiet and pretty gentle compared to the rest of us. But he still had the Donnahue temper that all of us had when we mad. Even though Isadora and Daniella had married into the family, they did the Donnahue name justice as when they got mad, they got really really mad.

Where I worked as an actor, Gwennie worked as a magazine editor while Strider is a lawyer and well, Isadora wasn't working at the moment due to her being pregnant and taking care of Phillip. Cameron worked in the real estate business while Daniella worked part time in a kindergarten. Emmett on the other hand, is still studying to be a doctor in a university.

Our family was often at times messy as hell. Gwennie and I were the ones always fighting and trying to one-up each other. It was like sibling rivalry. Emmett stayed out of family drama and was always a spectator.

Isadora and Gwennie fought at times while Daniella always became their intermediary and my two older brothers would alway stay out of it. Obviously, they didn't want to be part of the feud and be the new focus of their wives' anger.

It was quite hilarious seeing my two brothers try to get into their wives' good graces.

I sighed as soon bickering started in the kitchen as once again, Isadora and Gwennie fought and the shattering of glass sounded. Getting up from my seat, I entered the kitchen to diffuse the fight before any more of my plates got injured.

* * *

Later that night when all my family members had gone off, I contemplated on this situation with Emma.

She was right, I wanted to go out with her because she didn't want me. But that wasn't the only reason, I liked being around her. She was honest about how she felt about me and what she thought of me.

It was like a breath of fresh air. Most people would sugar coat the truth or keep it to themselves in fear of offending me because I'm Jack Donnahue. But I liked her honesty and her wittiness was something I enjoyed (even though it was aimed at me). Yay.

Also, her particular brand of humour amused me-dry humour. I also liked that she was straightforward and direct with me. Even if she didn't see me as something, I saw her as someone I wanted in my life like a friend. Because I knew I could count on her to give me an honest opinion on myself.

A grin formed on my face, Emma didn't say we couldn't be friends now did she?

* * *

A/N: Hi guys! I hope you like this chapter. And thank you so much for your lovely constructive criticism, I really appreciate it! But you guys will understand why Emma is so harsh and cold to Jack in the later chapters. Thanks so much for reading and and God bless all of you! Please vote and comment and give me your thoughts on the Donnahue family. If you have any questions, you can ask me! :)

Chapter 6-The Start Of A Friendship

Chapter 6-The Start Of A Friendship

Jack Donnahue's POV

"Would you want me to get you a cooler full of ice to treat the burn marks you're gonna get?"

I gave a glare to Max who was smirking in amusement. "No thanks. I can handle myself just fine."

"That's not what I saw the other day in her office. Because you were being set on fire from her tongue lashing." Max grinned and I rolled my eyes.

It has been almost week since I last saw Emma at the grocery store last Friday and for some strange reason, I was yearning to see her again. Maybe I was a sucker for punishment to want to get more blows to my ego. But whatever.

"This should work right?" I gestured to the two cups of coffee in the cup holder beside me as we drove to the museum.

Max shrugged as he stopped as the traffic lights turned red. "I have absolutely no idea. As far as I know, you've never done anything like this. And I don't think you have any actual female friends. And no, Isadora and Daniella don't count."

I shut my mouth in protest and groaned. "Why are females so hard to figure out?"

Max let out a bark of laughter and started the car once again as the lights turned green. "Hey aren't you Jack Donnahue, the ladies man?"

"Shut it Max! This is different!"

I scowled as Max bit back a grin and we drove in silence before I started unable to deal with the silence, "Are you sure butterscotch is okay? Not raspberry? I saw her getting both ice-cream flavours."

Max stifled a laugh, "Firstly too bad if she doesn't like it. I don't think coffee houses sell anything such as rapberry flavoured coffee. So butterscotch it is."

I groaned and slid on a cap and a pair of sunglasses, not bothering with the wig I had worn the last time because Emma looked like she wanted to laugh when she saw it on me.

"Here goes nothing." I mumbled and left the car and grabbed the two drinks with me and entered the museum.

The first person who spotted me was Roxanne the receptionist who beamed and nodded as I silently asked her if Emma was around. She gestured to the direction of Emma's office and I gave her a grateful smile before heading to Emma's office.

Luckily, I wasn't standing out and thus, I was able to walk around unnoticed. Entering the hallway that lead to Emma's office, I took a few deep breaths before knocking on Emma's door.

I have absolutely no clue on why I was so nervous. It wasn't going to be the first time I was rejected. Especially by Emma. Like Jesus, the number of rejections I received from her was probably the most I had in my life.

Hearing her voice telling whoever to come in, I exhaled deeply and entered. Immediately her hazel eyes watched me warily as she stared at me from behind her desk.

"Jack, what are you doing here?" She questioned, her eyes were narrowed and calculative.

I offered a small smile, "I came to see you."

"Why? I thought we made it clear that I wasn't going to go out with you."

I shrugged, "I know that. But I wanted to see you to ask something of you."

"Jack are you serious? This is getting a little annoying." Emma narrowed her eyes at me as she spoke, her voice held a hint of irritation. I knew she suspected that I wanted to ask her out again even though she had rejected me plenty of times and she was getting annoyed.

I gave an unrepentant grin and shoved my free hand into one of my pockets. "Is that a good thing or a bad thing?" I asked and mentally awarded myself with some bonus points at the sight of Emma's lips twitching before she broke into a smile.

"Damn you Jack." She mumbled under her breath and I smirked proudly. "I know. You're not the first to tell me that." I grinned and she sighed heavily before turning her attention back to me.

"Please, have a seat." She gestured to one of the chairs facing her and I eagerly sat down, pleased that she wasn't telling me to get out. "So? What did you want to talk about?" Emma questioned and I passed one of the two cups to her.

"This is a uh, an apology for annoying you last week and uhm a token of friendship?" I started with an awkward smile on my face.

"Friendship?" Emma asked disbelieving as she looked at me before glancing down at the cup of iced coffee on the table that I had given her. "You want to be friends with me? Even though I was pretty harsh to you?"

I nodded with a small grin on my face. "Yeah, I must be a sucker for punishment because I like that about you and I kinda deserved it." I said as I referred to the reason for wanting to ask Emma out. That was a huge jerk move.

Emma frowned and peered into the cup. "Is this coffee?"

I nodded and shrugged casually, "Yes. Butterscotch iced latte. I saw that you liked butterscotch and raspberry flavoured ice-cream but they don't have anything like raspberry coffee so I hope butterscotch is fine."

Emma bit her lip and fiddled with her fingers on the desk. "Oh, I'm really sorry Jack but I don't drink coffee."

Oh fuck. How the hell did I not think of that? I could feel my face fall and I forced a smile on my face, "Oh, it's alright then, I'll drink both."

A look of guilt flashed across Emma's face and she offered me a smile. "But, I love butterscotch. So I'll drink this. Just this time."

I grinned as Emma hesitantly sipped from the straw, her hazel eyes widening in surprise as she drank it. Setting the drink back on her desk, she beamed at me and admitted. "That was actually better than I thought it would be."

Shrugging, I sipped from my cup and sighed in contentment as the caffeine entered my body. "So friends?"

Emma studied me and she tilted her head before she questioned. "Why me? I'm sure you have other friends from your world."

I grinned. "You make me sound like an alien."

Emma shot me a flat stare and raised an eyebrow, not saying anything as she waited for me to continue with an expectant stare. I turned serious and ran my fingers through my hair.

"I like your honesty about your feelings and thoughts about me. It's quite refreshing and it's different-a good kind of different when I'm always surrounded by people who suck up to me because of who I am." I said seriously.

Emma raised an eyebrow before commenting dryly. "It's amazing how throughout that speech of yours, you managed to show your arrogant side."

I gave her an unrepentant grin and shrugged which faded into a serious expression. "I mean it Emma. I like that you don't care if I'm offended by your honesty. And it would be really nice if you were to be a friend that is honest and direct with me."

I said sincerely as possible, hoping that Emma could see how serious I was being. I continued, "Also, you don't seem like the type to try to get attention by being around me. And I like that. Because it's pretty funny when you run from it."

Emma studied me with inquisitive eyes and a serious expression before looking down at her drink. Her eyes met mine once more before she gave me a nod.

"Alright. But I don't want the paparazzi knowing about this." She stated firmly as she took another sip from the drink I bought. Relief and amusement filled my entire being as Emma agreed.

I grinned and cocked an eyebrow curiously, "Why are you so afraid of them? They're harmless. For the most part."

"Right." Emma shot me a disbelieving stare before sipping again, my eyes were fixed on those pink pouty lips enclosing around the tip of a straw-Jesus Jack! Get your thoughts sorted!

"I don't like my life being dissected by them and the public and I'm a very private person." She stated and tucked a curl behind her ear.

I nodded, I understood that. Not everyone was cut out for this life. The public and the reporters drew some people crazy. But I didn't mind. Too much. Because at times, it could get pretty annoying.

"Okay. Friends?" I shot her a playful smile and raised my hand for her to shake it. Emma sighed heavily and shook my hand reluctantly. "Friends."

Her small hand was almost enveloped in mine and it was warm as hell. "So? What do we do? Have coffee at a coffee house and go to each other's house?" I offered with a grin.

Emma rolled her eyes. "Please do not tell me that was a Friends reference."

I burst into laughter and shrugged my shoulders. "Yeah it is. I'm surprised Miss Greywood that you know what that is." I mocked playfully and Emma rolled her eyes.

"I do watch television."

I laughed at her deadpanned expression and mimicked a high school girl, "So what do you want to do now? Go shopping? Do our nails?"

Emma raised an eyebrow sceptically. "Right now, I'm seriously questioning your sexual preferences."

I glared at her. "I'll have you know that I'm totally straight. I asked you out remember? And that is what women do together right?" I argued, slightly offended. This was a huge blow to my male ego. Not that there was anything wrong with people who weren't straight but I was not! I like women.

A smirk curved on Emma's face as she stared at me with smugness on her face before she glanced at the stack of folders on her desk. "Well Jack, what do you really think females do when you go out together?"

"Have pillow fights during sleepovers-"

"No, we do not have those in our underwear." Emma cut me off and shot me a disapproving look. I slumped back into my seat and frowned and questioned. "Then what exactly do you even do during those?"

Emma scoffed and took another sip and this time, I restrained myself from looking at her mouth. "Watch movies, pig out on food, talk."

What. I had lived my whole life thinking that. "Really? That's a shocker." I muttered and continued. "Well, then why was my sister always so secretive when she had sleepovers with her friends?

Emma shrugged before asking curiously. "You have a sister?"

I snorted and shook my head. "Yes, and three brothers. Two older and one younger. My older brothers are married with children and my sister is engaged."

"Wow." Emma mouthed in awe before looking at the stack of folders on her desk. "Well Jack, unlike you, I do have work to get to."

I sat up straight and narrowed my eyes at her. "I do work you know. I'm an actor." I said defensively and Emma snorted. "Yeah. You just memorise lines, recite them and look pretty in front of the cameras."

Rolling my eyes, I scoffed and grabbed Emma's drink from her desk. "Take it back!"

Emma scoffed in response. "How old are you? Five?"

"No. Physically, twenty-nine. But mentally, six." I replied with a straight face on and watched in amusement as Emma tried not to laugh but failed and a laugh bubbled out of her.

"Damn you, Jack." She grumbled and I awarded myself more bonus points. Emma reached for her drink which was still in my grasp and frowned when I moved it away from her reach.

"Hey!" She protested and I grinned at her sneakily. "I thought you didn't like coffee."

She shot me a scowl before pursing her lips. "I don't but that is nice." She admitted and glared at me when she tried to take it back. "Seriously Jack! What kind of friend are you?"

I feigned anger and scoffed. "Oh please, I'm an awesome friend."

Emma glared at me and replied sharply. "I highly doubt it and right now, I'm really reconsidering this friendship." She said with a deadpanned tone and I gave in.

"Fine. Here's your coffee, Miss I-don't-like-coffee." I mumbled and Emma rolled her eyes as she tried not to smile. "Seriously how old are you?"

I grinned as I reminded her. "I told you earlier remember?" Emma rolled her eyes in response.

And this is how our friendship started.

* * *

A/N: Hi! Here is the next chapter as promised! Hope you guys love it! Let me know what you all think! Thanks so much for reading and please vote and comment! <3

Chapter 7-The Pick-Up Lines

Chapter 7-The Pick-Up Lines

Emmaline Heywood's POV

"Are you a magician? Because whenever I look at you, everyone else disappears."

I groaned and slapped my hand on my forehead. "That's lame." I said flatly and Jack grinned at me playfully before laughing at my expression.

"Do you sit in a pile of sugar? Cos' baby, you have a pretty sweet ass."

I frowned and tried to keep the smile off my face but failed and choked before giving in to laughing. "Jack! That was terrible!"

"Is your dad a baker? Because you have some nice buns." My jaw dropped at that and Jack gave me a shameless grin before erupting into raucous laughter. Hushing him before we attracted too much attention, I took another sip from my tea.

"Your body is 65% water and I'm thirsty."

I frowned and threw a fry at him. "Okay, that's disgusting. Jack frowned and scrunched up his face as he tried to come up with another line.

Right now, we were in a pretty cafe that was quite empty and we were seated in a corner booth. Jack was wearing his usual sunglasses and a cap but this time, the beard was back on. It had been a pretty hectic week so far and today was a Monday and Jack had appeared at the museum and suggested we go for lunch during my break.

I agreed reluctantly, still fearing that I could be captured hanging out with Jack by reporters but seeing the disguise Jack had on, he had reassured me that it was okay.

"Okay what about this? Do you live in a corn field? Because I'm stalking you."

I snorted and shot him a wry look. "You did stalk me when I was at the grocery store two weeks ago." I pointed out and Jack rolled his eyes, "No, I told you! I was there for coffee!" He insisted and I raised my eyebrows skeptically. "Sure." I mumbled.

"Okay, do you like Harry Potter? If so, you should open your Chamber of Secrets to let my Basilisk Slytherin."

I gaped at him in disbelief and Jack exploded into raucous laughter while I could only stare at him, "That was just plain appalling!"

Jack gave me a crooked smirk before breaking into a grin. "Well what about, 'You look so familiar... didn't we take a class together? I could have sworn we had chemistry."

I took another sip from my tea and shot back at him. "Are you sure you took Chemistry? You seem like the type to have dropped the subject after the first ten minutes of the very first lesson."

Jack glared at me and this time, it was he who threw a fry in my direction. I grinned at his offended expression and he shot me a flat look.

"Hey, you said you appreciated my honesty." I pointed out with a grin. "Regretting wanting to be friends with me?"

"No." Jack answered me sourly and stuffed a huge bite in his greasy burger while I frowned in distaste at it. I liked burgers but burgers with three kinds of meat in it? No.

Jack had ordered a burger called 'The Deluxe Triple Meat Burger' and I was still awed at the sight of a huge burger with a beef patty, bacon strips and chicken dripping with cheese.

"Don't you have to eat healthily to be in shape for your acting roles?" I questioned as I grimaced as Jack stuffed more of the burger into his mouth.

"Yeah, but I work out a lot. Want to see?" He offered with a smirk on his face with his brown eyes lit up from amusement.

I shot him a dry look and stated. "No."

Jack shrugged and sipped from his iced coffee. "Your loss."

"I wouldn't exactly consider that as a loss, more like a gain because I wouldn't have to sanitise my eyeballs."

He glared at me and I bit back a grin. "You're really boosting my ego here." He responded dryly and I simply shrugged as a response.

At times during the past week since Jack and I became friends, I had wondered if it was a smart idea in the first place. I had the taste of a perfect Hollywood life when I was younger but I had put that behind me and was now living a (happy) private one.

Jack Donnahue was a very well known and popular actor. If he was caught spending way too much time with me, the reporters would interpret me as his love interest and they would dissect my life piece by piece. Also, this time, I had Ella to think about.

I couldn't let any semblance of a normal childhood for her be ruined. Like how mine was. Hollywood was toxic and I was glad that I was out of it.

"Are you sure you don't want some? It's really really good." He grinned suggestively and for a moment, I wasn't sure if he was talking about the burger or...something else.

And looking at the mischievous glint in his eyes, I knew exactly what he was referring to. Pretending not to notice anything but wanted to make another jibe at him, I stared at him before commenting nonchalantly.

"I doubt it can be that good."

Jack narrowed his eyes at me before taking another bite of his burger. Inwardly, I high-fived myself and took another bite from my sandwich.

"I was talking about the burger."

I raised an eyebrow and replied once I've swallowed all the food in my mouth. "I know."

Jack made a face as he stuffed the remaining portion of the burger into his mouth while I watched with slight disgust. Was this the real Jack Donnahue that reporters and fans never knew?

Because good god, the press would have a field day if they knew how Jack behaved when the cameras weren't around.

I studied him a little, wondering what the world saw in him that made him so famous and well liked. He had dark brown hair (that looked pretty soft), good facial features and dark brown eyes. He was pretty tall (my guess, about six feet) and pretty muscled.

He was good looking but then, most actors and actresses in Hollywood were. But I figured that it was his personality and character that made Jack so well liked. He had a way of making you laugh and talk. He wasn't a jerk and he was pretty friendly.

Polishing the rest of my sandwich, I sighed in satisfaction and leaned against my chair and wiped my mouth with the napkin given. "Roxanne told me you're currently filming a movie. What kind of movie is it?"

Jack nodded. "Yeah, a romantic one just in time for Valentine's Day. I'm the male lead and the actress Rachel Morgan is the female lead."

I wrinkled my nose, romantic films? Ugh, no. It was highly unrealistic and just plain ridiculous. Women always acted silly in those movies and the men are the type that has it all in life.

"What? You don't like those?" Jack frowned and I shrugged and glanced down at my iced tea. "No. Not really no."

"Why not? Do you have something against romance? You don't like flowers and you don't like romantic films." Jack sputtered in disbelief as he gaped at me.

I shrugged in response and answered as a matter of factly, "Flowers are a waste of money. It'll wilt and die in less than a week. Romantic movies are unrealistic and pointless. In reality, not all guys get the girl and vice versa.

And I believe that romantic films showcase the worst in both males and females." I finished and took another sip of my tea.

Jack stared at me, stunned and his jaw worked for quite a while as he tried to think of a response. "What is wrong with you? And why are you so practical about everything?" He sputtered and I shrugged.

"I believe It's a good trait to have." I stated and stifled a laugh at Jack's gobsmacked expression.

"Or you're jaded in all things romantic." He mumbled under his breath and I rolled my eyes. "Think whatever you like, but I think romance is ridiculous."

Jack shook his head vigorously. "This just shows that you haven't been romanced properly and neither have you watched good romance films. It's settled. We'll have a movie marathon at your house or mine."

I coughed and choked a little on my drink and questioned quickly. "What? No!" No to having a movie marathon with Jack and disbelief at the fact that he accused me of not being romanced. When the truth was I had enough of those to fill up my entire lifetime.

No no no no. I didn't have time for that. Well, the correct reasoning is that Ella would be home and my house is decorated with pictures of my brother and her. I could not have Jack around to see all of that and nor was I removing them.

I absolutely did not want to be alone with Jack in his home. No way, things that I didn't want could happen and Jack was a terrible flirt. Also, his stalkers, fans and reporters could be around and word would get out.

"Why not?" He frowned as he pouted and I scoffed in reply, "I don't like people coming to my house and messing everything up." I gave this as an excuse. While it may not be the real reason, it was a reason nonetheless.

"I promise I won't touch anything." Jack says seriously and I would have taken him for real if I had not spotted the mischievous glint in his brown eyes.

"Liar." I called him out and he gave me a shameless grin.

"Alright, we'll have this discussion later. Do you have any siblings?" He questioned as he dipped a fry in both ketchup and chilli sauce.

My nose wrinkled at that and I questioned warily, "Why do you want to know?"

Jack frowned as he replied, "Because isn't that what people ask their friends?"

I shook my head and forced a smile on my face. I hated talking about my family. It was messed up. Forcing myself to relax, I nodded. "Yes, a brother." I said quietly, not wanting to divulge anything else. I wasn't this forth coming with information about myself.

Sometimes, I wondered if Jack knew who I was but he seemed clueless about my situation. And I liked it that way. "So what's his name? Is he older or younger?"

"Older." I said shortly as I ignored his first question and I desperately wanted this topic of conversation to be over. But of course, Jack couldn't take hints well. "What about your parents?"

I pursed my lips and shifted uncomfortably. "I don't want to talk about them." I replied stiffly and finally Jack got my hint and he nodded his head awkwardly.

"I have four siblings, two sisters-in-law and a soon-to-be brother-in-law. Two older brothers, a younger sister and a younger brother and two nephews and a niece." He grinned and I raised my eyebrows.

"That's a really big family. It must be fun." I offered and Jack shrugged. "Yeah, but it can be crazy. What's your favourite colour?"

I blinked at the sudden change of topic. "White. Why do you want to know so much about me?" I questioned a little warily and Jack shrugged and raised an eyebrow.

"Mine's orange if you were wondering. And we're friends aren't we? We're supposed to know things about each other." He grinned and I nodded my head unsurely.

Once again, the thought of being friends with Jack made me wonder if it was a good idea.

"So? If you don't like films with the romance genre, what sort do you like to watch?" Jack prompted and I glanced at my watch, seeing that I still had thirty minutes more before I had to go back to work.

The director of the museum was one of the few people who knew my real name and allowed me to be registered as Emma Greywood. He was like the father figure while his wife was like a mother figure. Something that I never had while growing up.

"I like thriller films." I answered and Jack shook his head disapprovingly. "Okay, we have to get you started on our planned movie marathon."

I could feel a frown appear on my face at that. I really did not recall agreeing to anything of that sort, but I couldn't be bothered to argue with Jack. He was a persistent sort. I'd rather let him think that I agreed than saying it verbally.

"Just as long as I don't have to watch anything that you acted in."

"What? Why not?"

"It'll be odd. And from what I know, you mostly act in romance films." I answered and Jack shot me a disgruntled expression.

He crossed his arms and sulked. "That may be true, but I do act in other films too!" I didn't bother replying and let my gaze remained fixed on my drink if not my eyes would wander to his muscular arms as they strained against the sleeves of his shirt.

I had a thing for muscular and lean guys. Keyword: had. Sighing, I straightened up in my seat and glanced at my watch once more to check the time. "I got to go back to work soon."

Jack nodded. "Alright, pass me your phone." He ordered and laid his palm open.

"Why?"

"So that I can have your number." He said with a straight face though laughter was in those brown eyes of his.

Narrowing my eyes, I tilted my head to study him. "This isn't another pick-up line right?"

Jack rolled his eyes. "No, but aren't friends supposed to have each other's cellphone numbers?" I eyed his outstretched hand and slipped my phone on it reluctantly. I watched Jack warily as he pressed his number into my phone with a sly grin on his face.

Once he passed it back to me, I pressed the lock button of my phone and choked back a snort. "Seriously, you put your face as my wallpaper?"

Jack burst into laughter and I fought back an amused smile and covered it with an exasperated sigh, scrolling through my contacts, I stopped and stared at Jack's contact and the name he put for himself.

"My new BFF?" I read out and asked incredulously and Jack exploded into more laughter.

Rolling my eyes, I stuffed my phone back into my pocket. "I have to go now." I stated and Jack nodded. "Alright. But want to hear something before you go?"

I gestured for him to go ahead and he flashed a sly grin on his face.

"I wish you were my little toe, so that I can bang you on every piece of furniture in my house."

"Jack!"

* * *

A/N: Here is the next chapter! I hope you guys love it! Let me know your thoughts! And please vote and comment! Thanks so much for reading! <3

Chapter 8-The Phone Calls

Chapter 8-The Phone Calls

Jack Donnahue's POV

"Okay! Get in your places!" The director yelled and I stepped into the character that I was playing, Winston Anderson while Rachel, the actress who was playing my love interest, Karen Wilson got into position.

The movie that we were filming was about a man who went off for college, left his girlfriend behind with a promise that he was coming back. However, he had gotten into a car accident and had amnesia. Five years later, he went back to his hometown and encounters his old girlfriend who thought that he had abandoned her.

And now, his girlfriend is engaged but helps him to remember. Gradually, he falls back in love with her but leaves her be as she is going to get married. However, Karen played by Rachel broke off the engagement and goes after Winston.

However, Winston feels that he isn't enough for her and leaves. Two weeks later, he finds Karen at his doorstep and they end up together.

Oh hell, the movie did sound pretty unrealistic and ridiculous. Emma's views were rubbing off onto me. Damn it to hell Emma! I cursed.

"One, two, three, action!" The director yelled and immediately, I caressed Rachel's cheek. "I can't believe you're here." I say softly and she shut her eyes and leaned into my touch.

"Winston I love you. I want to be with you." She declared and I frowned. "What about Jason?"

Rachel sighed, "I broke things off him. It wasn't fair to him when I was in love with you. I love you Winston. Be it here or our hometown, I want to be with you."

I knew it was the big kiss scene and I stepped closer to Rachel and murmur softly. "I love you too Karen." With that, I pressed my lips against hers.

Even though I had done this countless of times before, it felt...weird. Rachel's hands gripped onto me and I held her waist as we kissed.

"And cut! Thanks everybody! We're done for the day!" The director called out and I quickly pulled away from Rachel. The kiss left me feeling weirded out but I brushed it aside.

Running my fingers through my hair, I left the set but got stopped by the director who grinned at me. "Great job Jack. That was actually the last scene. The producers and I have agreed to skip the last scene. You're done."

He grinned and patted me on the back and without waiting for a response, he left and started barking out orders. I shrugged and went back to my trailer and Max started following behind me.

As I walked back to my trailer, I gave small smiles to those who walked passed and greeted me. Once we were in private, Max raised an eyebrow and questioned. "What's with that face you have on?"

I shrugged and grabbed another bottle of iced coffee, "What face?"

"The weird one, I thought you'll be happy. After all, you'll have about a three months break before you have to start filming your new movie." Max started and I nodded.

"I know..." I trailed off and my mind went back to the kiss with Rachel and I forced it away from my mind. Turning to Max, I questioned with a straight face. "Max, can I have a very honest opinion from you?"

He shrugged, "Sure what?"

"What do you think about romance movies?"

Max raised his eyebrows in surprise, "Uhm, they're movies that I would not watch."

I frowned. "Why not? Doesn't everybody watch it?"

Max frowned and stared at me. "Uhm no. I think people watch them because you're in it. And that because you're mostly shirtless in it."

I made a face at that and rolled my eyes. "Do you think this movie being filmed is ridiculous and unrealistic?"

"Where is this coming from?" Max asked bewildered and I shot him a pointed glare for him to answer the question. "Yes. I do. But I'm sure other people like this sort of thing."

"Damn it. Emma's right." I muttered under my breath and Max burst into laughter. "That's what this is all about? Oh, someone should hand that girl an award. Never have I seen you second guess your choices and yourself because you know, your ego is out of this world."

"Thanks Max." I uttered dryly and if it was possible Max burst into more laughter at my expense.

Turning away from him, I stared down at my phone and frowned a little. Emma hadn't called. Not once. Even though I had given her my number. Didn't friends call each other and hung out?

I didn't know but something about her made me very curious. Seeing her just two days ago made me wonder about her constantly. I did notice that she was very closed off about herself, rarely offering information or tiny details about her personal life.

And that made me all the more curious. People loved talking about themselves. Everyone except Emma it would seem. My fingers itched to call her but I refrained myself from doing that. I wasn't some teenage boy yearning for his crush.

I was Jack Donnahue, and well, I didn't like Emma that way. But I was curious as hell about her. I only knew that she worked in a museum, her favourite colour was white (how boring), she had a brother (again, older or younger?) and she was smart as hell.

She was also witty, sarcastic, cautious and yet she hated reporters. She also hated romantic movies and flowers. But anything about her personal life? She would have her guard up.

To be honest, I had contemplated texting her but I suspected that she would reply with one word answers. Again, a first time for me. Since I was Jack Donnahue.

"Just call her. Your thumb keeps hovering over her contact. And did she even allow you to take that?" Max questioned as he eyed the photo I had taken of Emma (without her knowing) as she looked out of the window of the cafe just the other day.

Seeing her various expressions when I told her my pick-up lines made me want to burst into laughter.

"Of course not, she would have made me delete it." I stated and stared at said photo. My eyes lingering on her profile as she sipped on her drink.

Out of sudden before I could stop him, Max pressed the call icon and my phone started displaying the picture when I called someone. "What the fuck Max!"

Beside me Max started laughing and I started freaking out and before I could end the call, Emma picked it up. "Hello Jack?" She greeted and I quickly put the phone against my ear and glared at Max to shut up.

"Uh, hi!" I greeted and Max doubled up into silent laughter at my awkward greeting.

"Hi, is there a reason for calling me?" She questioned and I wanted to kick myself. "No, just wanted to say hi and ask how are you doing."

There was a moment of silence and Emma answered, "You just saw me two days ago, and yes, I'm doing fine."

I must have made a face and Max grabbed my phone and made it to speaker mode. I glared at him before remembering that Emma was waiting for my response. "Uh yeah. Have you changed your wallpaper?"

Emma sighed heavily through the phone. "Jack, you seriously can't be calling me for this. And yes, I have. Seeing your face in my phone is going to make me die early. Not because you're good looking but because of the fright it will give me."

I cracked a grin at that and laughed, "Well, I did expect that to be changed but what about my contact? Did you change that?"

"No. I couldn't be bothered nor did I have the time. I'm sure my best friend would be a little annoyed but he'll deal." She stated and I heard some rustling sounds as if she was doing paperwork.

My ears picked up on the word 'he'. "So what are you doing now?" I questioned and Emma answered. "Actual work and I say that because I don't really think acting can be considered as that."

As Emma stated that so casually, Max lit up and burst into more silent laughter, obviously pleased that Emma shared his views on my career.

"Emma, I told you, acting is an actual job." I repeated and she snorted delicately. "Right. Anyway, I got to go-" Emma's voice got cut off and a male voice answered.

"Is this the dashing Jack Donnahue?"

I frowned and answered. "Uh, yes. Who is this?" In the background noise, I can hear Emma telling off whoever was holding onto the phone.

"Oh, this is Zachary Richmond, your future brother-in-law. Gwen didn't want me meeting you but I thought I'll take the initiative to say hi."

My eyes widened in recognition and I grinned and for some strange reason, relief bloomed in the pit of my stomach, "Oh hi! Yeah, that sounds like Gwennie. I didn't know you're friends with Emma." I answered with a grin (even though he couldn't see me).

Zachary laughed. "Yeah, I'm her first best friend, and from looking at her phone, you're her second. Anyway, I just wanted to tell you that Emma thinks you're really hot and that she likes your muscles and she has seen all the movies you acted in."

Emma started yelling angrily and I could hear her through the phone that her manner of speaking was still as sophisticated. "Oh really?" I smirked, knowing that it was all untrue and that Zach only wanted to make Emma uncomfortable and embarrassed.

"Yeah, she even told me that at night, she thinks about you when-" Zach started and got cut off as Emma said quite sharply.

"That is quite enough Zachary Richmond!"

Zach burst into laughter and I couldn't help but grin. Rustling noises and yells could be heard and I guessed that Emma was forcing Zach to return the phone to her.

I waited patiently and I could feel Max watching me with an amused grin on his face. "Ugh, hey Jack, I'll talk to you later, I got to go."

I nodded and shrugged, "Yeah sure, not a problem." I answered and Emma hung up before I could.

I couldn't help but grin to myself and I looked up to see Max studying me with an amused smirk. "What?" I questioned and Max shrugged. "Nothing. By the way, set security called while you were on the phone. Venice is here to see you."

Clenching my jaw, I frowned, "Why?"

Venice Anderson was a model who I've gotten to know briefly and people thought we were together but nothing ever happened between us. I didn't particularly like her attitude or her behaviour.

Max shrugged and Venice burst into the room with her cloud of perfume announcing her arrival. Max made a face and Venice scowled at him before turning to me. "Hi Jack!" She greeted and leaned forward to kiss me but I moved away.

"Uh, hi. What are you doing here?" I questioned and discreetly moved to stand beside Max. Venice sighed and tossed her auburn curls behind her shoulder and gave me a seductive pout. "I'm here to see you."

Beside me, Max coughed and I rolled my eyes, knowing what he was referring to. This was what Emma must have felt the first few times I went to see her.

"Uh, but why?"

She tilted her head, "You told me you'll see me again the other day at Tom's party. Here I am."

Truthfully, I had told her that so that she would leave me alone that night. But I should've told her that I didn't want her that way directly. It was literally biting me in the ass.

"Look Venice, I have to tell you this. I just want to be... friends with you."

"Friends with benefits?" She perked up and my eyes widened. Hell no!

"No, just friends, and I gotta go. Very busy with filming and stuff." Max snorted, knowing that was lie considering I just finished shooting the last scene and Venice scowled. "Fine. Whatever." With that, she stalked out of my trailer, however the scent of her perfume still lingered.

"Ugh." I mumbled and fanned the air around me. "I'm surprised you didn't take her up for her offer." Max uttered with a look of curiosity on his face.

I shrugged and brushed him off. "No way. She's not my type and she scares me."

Max chuckled, "Of course, when a certain Emma Greywood has your attention."

I turned to him and shot him a pointed stare. "Emma and I aren't like that. We're just friends."

"Sure, and I'm the Easter bunny. Just let me know when you guys get together so I can say I told you so." He grinned and I rolled my eyes and ignored him and left the trailer.

Later that night, as I got into bed, I remembered that Emma said that I could call her. Reaching for my phone, I waited eagerly for her to pick up. Hearing the other end pick up. I grinned and waited to hear Emma's voice but instead, another voice sounded.

"Hello?"

It was a voice of a young girl and my jaw dropped in shock and I quickly hung up.

What the hell?

* * *

A/N: Hi guys, here is the next chapter. I hope you guys love it and please vote and comment! It'll mean the world to me. Thanks so much for reading and hopefully, I'll get a chapter for TOK by today or latest tomorrow.

Chapter 9-The Confusion

Chapter 9-The Confusion

Jack Donnahue's POV

What the hell?

Emma had a kid?

My mind had been stuck on that fact the whole of last night, thus not allowing me to sleep at all. Was that what Emma meant when she said she had responsibilities? Or could I be overthinking about things and blowing them out of proportion?

I knew it was common for some people to be single parents but Emma? She didn't seem like the type. And then again, I may be jumping to conclusions.

I groaned and sat up in my bed. I was going crazy with all these thoughts about Emma. Was that her daughter on her phone? It seemed quite likely. The fact that she didn't want anything to do with me and reporters was a dead giveaway because that's what any parent would do.

I know I should feel relieved that I had managed to barely avoid something like this. I wasn't that great around kids. With my niece and two nephews, I was awkward around them. Unless they asked me to teach them poker or something.

But instead of pure relief, I was just confused. And a little disappointed. Not because Emma had a kid but because she didn't tell me.

I had to get to the bottom of this.

I put on a pair of sunglasses and quickly dressed and placed a beanie on my head as a disguise (sort of) and left for the museum. It was about noon when I reached and before I could exit my car, I spotted Emma getting into hers and driving off before I could speak to her.

Debating if I should follow after her, I gave in to being stupid and did. To be honest, I wasn't thinking clearly and I followed Emma through the traffic and stopped and got out of my car.

Oh Jesus, she was picking her kid up? I stared at the kindergarten that was painted in warm colours that made it look warm and inviting for the students (I guessed).

I hesitated on staying and debated if I should quickly leave. Deciding on that, I turned back to my car and stopped when Emma called out, "Jack?"

Oh fuck. I forced on a smile and turned to her, "Hey Emma..." I trailed off awkwardly and met her wary gaze. "What are you doing here?" She questioned, her eyes darting to me and to the kindergarten building a few metres in front of us.

"Uh..." I trailed off, not knowing how to answer.

She gave me an expectant gaze. Her light brown eyes were narrowed and her hair was in a disarray. I quickly forced myself to continue. "I called your phone yesterday and a young girl picked up-your daughter? And I followed you here from the museum." I finished and now Emma's face had a blank expression on.

An awkward silence started and I felt annoyance creep up on me. Why didn't Emma tell me that she had a kid? Weren't we friends? It wasn't like I was going to judge her based on her having a kid. I mean hell, look at my own family. I was hardly in a position to judge her.

"Why the hell didn't you tell me you had a daughter? Aren't we friends?" I asked, glad that my sunglasses was on so that Emma couldn't see the annoyance and irritation showing in my eyes.

However, I guessed I must have done a poor job in masking those feelings in my tone because Emma narrowed her eyes dangerously.

"Firstly, I've known you for almost two months. I wouldn't exactly consider it a long enough friendship to spill secrets. After all, you have reporters after you and I still hardly know you that much. Why would I tell you my whole life story?"

She said harshly, her brown eyes glaring at me and I remained silent before she continued. "Secondly, Ella is my niece, her dad-my brother is in a coma in the hospital and I'm her guardian. Not that it is any of your business." She said angrily, eyes flashing and her lips were pressed together into a thin line. However, I could see her brown eyes glimmering in pain and guilt hit me like a truck.

My jaw dropped and I yelled at my brain to come up with a response and when I did, I couldn't speak because at that moment, a girl who was about five years old ran over to Emma and shouted what Emma had confirmed.

"Aunt Emma!" She shouted and hugged Emma's leg before looking up at me curiously with her big brown eyes. Looking at me, she shyly ducked her head behind Emma's legs while peering up at me.

I stared at her awkwardly and plastered on a small smile. "Hi there." Ella stared at me and gave me a small toothy grin before turning to Emma and pointing to a cut on her knee.

Emma sighed and stroked her hair and promised to buy some raspberry gummy candies for her. My ears perked up at that. So it wasn't Emma who liked raspberry flavoured ice-cream, it was her niece.

With that, Emma straightened before bending down to take Ella's hand and gazed at me with a blank expression on her face.

"Goodbye Jack." She said tonelessly before walking off with Ella beside her leaving me staring at their retreating forms.

More guilt pooled in me and it felt like a punch was thrown into my gut. I certainly had no right to demand answers from Emma like that. No wonder she didn't like talking about her brother, my mind recalling to that incident in the cafe where I had told her pick up lines.

Her brother was in a coma. I felt like an A-class prick. If any of my siblings were in one, I wouldn't like talking about it at all. Much less to anyone I've known for about only two months. I was irrational and I guess I was being stupid to handle this incident this way.

I knew I had to apologize but how? I didn't know where Emma stayed. My mind flickered to her best friend Zach, also known as Gwennie's fiancé. A grin curved onto my face and I called my sister.

Much later, I was standing in front of Emma's door, a bag full of raspberry gummy sweets in my hand. Okay Jack, pull your nerves together and knock!

Gwennie had passed her phone to Zach who had promptly given me Emma's address but also warning me not to hurt his best friend. And

before I had arrived, I had gone to the grocery store to get some sweets for
Ella.

And here I was standing in front of her house. Okay. Just fucking knock!
I gave myself a pep talk and with my fist raised to knock, the door opened
and Emma stared at me with a blank expression on her face.

* * *

Emmaline Heywood's POV

How dare he? How bloody dare he!

I hid my rising anger as Ella skipped towards our home with a big grin
on her face. Entering my apartment, my eyes stopped at the picture of my
brother and I. It was one of those pictures that made you stop and wonder
what was so funny.

That picture was taken when both Theo and I were twenty-one and he had
finally got away from our mother's controlling thumb. We had celebrated
in his home with loads of ice-cream and alcohol. Seeing that I was already
out of the family, it didn't matter to me when my mother had shouted at
my brother that she refused to lose her only child.

However, hearing that stung but I had straightened my resolve because I
knew what I was getting into when I left when I was sixteen.

I sighed wistfully as memories of that perfect night swarmed through my
head. Pushing those away for now, I turned to Ella who was making a mess
in the living room with her toys. I forced a smile on my face and went to
get lunch ready and I tried not to think about Jack.

Honestly, we were only friends for about two months and and him pulling
that friendship card was ridiculous. Sure I would be a little mad if I was in
his shoes. But he had absolutely no right to demand things from me.

I set my lips into a thin line and continued stirring the pasta sauce in the pot while keeping an ear out if Ella was up to any mischief.

Of course I had told Ella who her father was but she only referred to him as Theo. And obviously, she knew who her mother was. I hated her with every fibre in my being. Ella had cried the very first night she had stayed with me. Those words she had said had haunted me to this very day.

"Mommy said I was a mistake and wanted me to go away because I wasn't s'posed to be there."

I shuddered and gritted my teeth at the thought of that vile woman. Peering into the living room to check on Ella, I frowned when my phone started ringing. "What do you want Zach?"

My best friend's voice sounded out cheerfully as he started to ramble aimlessly before dropping the news that Jack Donnahue was dropping by my place as he had given him my address. With that, my arse of a best friend hung up and left me gaping at my phone.

Panic thrummed through my veins and my mind ran through what I had to do. No one had ever entered my apartment except for Zach and Theo. Not even my own parents. If Jack came over, there was an extremely high risk of him entering and seeing the pictures of Theo Heywood, a very famous actor.

Knowing that Jack was extremely charming when he wanted things to go his way, I let out an angry sigh and plotted to meet up with Zach's fiancée and dish out on all of Zachary Richmond's dirty secrets.

Quickly, I took down the photos of Theo and I and placed them in my bedroom before locking my bedroom door. Just as I did that, someone rang the doorbell.

I pressed my lips into a thin line and turned to see Ella peering at me curiously because well, we never have guests over. Theo had a key that he could enter whenever he wanted, Zach didn't bother ringing the bell, instead he would shout for me to open it (being the obnoxious best friend he was). I gave her a reassuring smile before opening the door warily.

The sight of Jack Donnahue greeted me and I forced myself to not admire how good he looked in a pair of jeans and a simple black shirt with sunglasses and a beanie on. Which in my opinion was ridiculous seeing that the weather was pretty warm.

"Jack." I greeted coolly before continuing. "How may I help you?" I questioned a little coldly and made sure the door wasn't opened all the way.

He shuffled his feet under my cool stare and sighed. "Emma, I'm sorry for earlier. I had no right to demand things from you that you're not ready to say and well, I'm sorry for being an absolute prick about it. I'm sorry about your brother too." Jack offered unsurely and I sighed while remaining silent.

I knew my silence was making the situation more tense and to my pleasure, Jack started shifting his weight from one foot to the other as he waited for me to say something due to my lack of response.

Seeing that it was slowly killing him because well, Jack Donnahue really was getting all fidgety and was soon to wear holes in my doormat, I sighed once more before nodding a little.

"It's fine. I don't talk about him a lot." I said quietly and continued. "I'm sorry about not telling you about Ella. I hope you understand why. She's just a kid that shouldn't be around anything from Hollywood."

I could see Jack relax a little as I spoke and he nodded. "Yeah. If I was in your shoes, I wouldn't want me to be anywhere near a kid."

I shrugged and commented dryly. "I don't know, I assume that your best friend - if you have one - is a kid as well considering that both your mental ages are about the same."

Jack rolled his eyes at my snarky comment but I could see a hint of a smile on his handsome face. "Really Em, you wound me with your hurtful comments."

I raised an eyebrow at the nickname he had given. Em? Deciding not to comment on it, I sighed and shoved one of my hands into the pockets of my jeans. "I'm really sorry about not telling you about her."

Jack nodded and shrugged before bursting into a bright grin. "It's okay. I'm sorry about whatever I said. I'm not that mean or pushy."

I scoffed under my breath and Jack shot me a little glare. "I'm not pushy!" He obviously knew what I meant when I had scoffed.

Clearing his throat, his face transformed into the bright grin he had on earlier. "Anyway, we're friends aren't we? You know everything about me and now I know everything about you."

I tensed a little at that. Technically that was true. Emmaline Grey Heywood no longer existed. Maybe except in government records but other than that, she was gone. So yes, Jack was right.

"Yes. Friends." I forced a smile on my face, wondering why there was a tiny hint of guilt burning in the pit of my stomach. Forcing that feeling away, I raised an eyebrow when I noticed that Jack had a grocery bag in his hand.

"What's that?" I gestured towards the bag.

He blinked and his expression turned a little sheepish. "Oh this? It's uh raspberry candy for your niece if that's okay with you of course."

I nodded a little hesitantly and Jack brightened up, "So I take it that I can meet her?"

I blinked. "What? When did you ask that?" I questioned a little anxiously. This is something that I did not expect. At all. Especially from Jack.

Oh dear god.

"When I said I had candy for her." Jack answered as he grinned. Looking at him, I pursed my lips as I weighed the possible pros and cons of Jack meeting Ella.

There could be no harm in this could it? Jack knew my reasons and I knew him well enough that he would respect them. Studying him a tab bit longer, I reluctantly nodded before opening the door wider for him to enter. But before I let him enter, I spun around and questioned. "Why do you want to meet her anyway?"

Jack gave me a shameless grin. "Because she's a part of your life and the other person in your life besides me who is vying for your attention."

I could only blink at that as I wordlessly let him enter my home. "So this is what your house looks like." He mumbled as he looked around curiously.

Turning him away, I spotted Ella looking at Jack curiously. I quickly made introductions and in no time, Jack and Ella were playing together with her dolls and both were snacking on the candy that Jack brought.

Looking at them, I could feel my insides twisting a little. Ella was the closest thing I had left of my brother. If he woke up at all. I steadied myself at the thought of him and pushed those thoughts back. I know he would wake up but I just didn't know when.

Seeing Ella bossing Jack around made me grin a little. Who knew Jack was great with kids?

* * *

A/N: Hi guys! Here is the next update! Yes, I know that some of you feel that Emma is really harsh and cold and well, the reason why her character is this way will be revealed in the later chapters. I hope you guys loved it! And please give a vote and a comment and I'll really appreciate it if you didThanks so much for reading and I love you all!

Chapter 10-The Questioning

Chapter 10-The Questioning

Jack Donnahue's POV

"So, I managed to get the name of the girl who outsmarted you and it's a bloody good thing Zach's her best friend if not you'll never tell me all about it!"

Gwennie almost shouted as we were led to our table in the restaurant and I thanked my lucky stars that it was quite empty seeing that it was odd hours.

Beside her, was her fiancé - Zachary Richmond. Also known as Emma's best friend. Zach had finally convinced Gwennie to meet up with me together for lunch seeing that I was the only family member who had yet to meet her fiancé.

And that was what brought us here. "Gwennie..." I glared at her. "Would you lower your voice?"

My sister sighed and tossed her blond locks behind her shoulder. "So come on, you went to her house yesterday. How was it?"

I glared at the inquisitive expression on both Zach and Gwennie's faces. "Isn't this meeting with the both of you is to be about you guys getting married? Why the hell am I being questioned?"

Gwennie scoffed and crossed her arms. "Don't bother acting all protective brother-like. Cameron and Strider already did that. Now I want to know about this Emma girl. Zach won't tell me much but since you're quasi-friends with her, maybe both of you will give me more insight." She announced and shot a little glare at Zach who shrugged in response without shrinking from Gwennie's glare.

Already, that won me over. Whichever male that wasn't afraid of Gwennie when she was being all snobby and demanding was good enough. Because hell, that also meant that he wouldn't bow down to every wish and demand my impulsive sister had.

"Spit it out Jack. I don't have all day."

I glared at her and Zach stifled a laugh before taking one of Gwennie's hands into his and intertwined their fingers. "Gwen, let your brother have a breather. Anyway Jack, I hoped you used the little tidbit I had given you to your full advantage because Emma chewed my ear out for that."

I broke into a grin at that, the image of Emma telling Zach off could be pictured in my head immediately. Her hazel eyes would be narrowed and her lips would be pressed into a thin line while she would be drumming her fingers against a hard surface. I had noticed these telltale signs when she was displeased with something.

"Well, I did. I met Ella." I offered and Zach raised an eyebrow before nodding approvingly. "Oh what do you think?"

"She's an amazing kid. She has a lot of dolls though." I answered with a bright grin as the little girl with blonde pigtails ordered me around with her toys. Emma obviously did a great job in bringing her up.

"Who's Ella? Her kid?" Gwennie questioned curiously as her eyes darted between Zach and I.

"She's Emma's niece." Zach answered smoothly and once again, I noticed that Zach was being vague with the details just like Emma had been doing.

Gwennie shot me a surprised look. "You played with her? Wow Jack, never thought that you would go after someone who is raising a kid. Impressive. You seem to have grown up." She added sweetly and I rolled my eyes at her.

Seems that Gwennie and Emma had something in common. And that was making sly little snarky comments about me. "It's not like that. Emma and I are just friends."

Gwennie let out a disbelievingly snort. "Yeah right. I'm a lesbian then."

Zach chuckled and gave her a sly grin. "Why didn't you tell me? We could have a threesome."

I gagged at that. The image that sprung into my mind was disgustingly revolting. As a brother, I certainly did not need to know about anything relating to my sister's sex life. An involuntary shiver went down my spine and Gwennie burst into laughter.

"Zach! We're giving my brother the chills." Zach wiggled his eyebrows at me and I made a face in reply.

Gwennie waved her hand dismissively, "Alright enough about Zach and I. So who's Ella's parents?"

"Her brother." Zach answered (vaguely again) and Gwennie frowned. "What happened to him? Of course I'm assuming something must have happened to him seeing that Emma is her guardian."

"Coma." Zach replied once more and again, I noticed that Zach cut his answers short and vague when a question about Emma's background was asked.

Hmmm. Interesting.

"So Jack what is Emma like?" Gwennie prompted and I groaned before admitting reluctantly because her best friend was just right there!

"She's really smart and funny." That was all I offered because again, Emma's best friend is just sitting opposite me with a knowing smirk on his face.

To be honest, those two words that I used was not all that could describe Emma Greywood. Beautiful, witty, caring, loyal, and well amazing was what I'd use.

Gwennie snorted again, what exactly did Zach see in that? "Yeah right. Jack you light up when you talk about her. Like now." She pointed out flatly and I didn't realise that I had a stupid shit-eating grin on my face.

The moment I did realise that, I quickly pulled my face into a flat expression and glared at Gwennie. "It is what it is. And Emma and I are just friends. That's it. Now shut up and eat the food that you ordered. Oh wait a minute, you can't. Seeing that you didn't order anything so that you can fit into your wedding dress."

Zach sucked in a breath and slumped into his seat and watched me with a little worry on his face.

"How dare you!" Gwennie shrieked and was moments away from lunging over the table to strangle me with her bare hands when an amused voice spoke up.

"Huh, Emmett really did give us the right address. Because Gwennie is about to attack Jack."

I groaned in annoyance as Isadora and Daniella sat with us with smug cat-like grins on their pretty faces. God must really hate me to give me siblings along with their nosey spouses.

"Hi Jack and Zach. Gwennie, knock it off. Daniella and I want to hear more about this Emma girl that Jack is mooning after." Isadora announced and I glared at her and Daniella's nosiness.

How is she even sitting down gracefully with an eight month old pregnant belly still astounds me. "Wipe that glare off your face. I really have to give this girl a trophy seeing that she keeps rejecting you."

"For the bloody last time! We're just friends!" I said exasperatedly. Turning to Zach, I gave him a disbelieving stare. "Are you really sure you want to be tied to all of them for the rest of your life? It's not too late to call of the engagement."

"I HATE YO-" Gwennie started and Zach covered her mouth with his hand. "I'm sure, I love your family and Gwennie is my everything."

All rage and snarling from Gwennie disappeared the moment Zach said that and she and him started a snogging session which both Isadora and Daniella cooed at while I made gagging sounds.

Was I the only one who was disturbed with the sight of my sister kissing someone? Looking at my family members, I groaned and rubbed my face with my hands in annoyance. Apparently yes.

"Alright both of you, enough. I'm here to hear more about Jack's love life or well the lack of it." Daniella ordered before giving me a knowing grin.

I clenched my jaw, wishing that I hadn't even agreed to this. I had only thought that this was about to meet Zach because he was Gwennie's fiancé. If I had known I was about to be ambushed by all the females in my family (excluding my niece) I wouldn't even turn up for this.

"Jack! Get on with it!" Isadora pushed and waved her hand for the waiter so she could order a drink or whatever she wanted.

"What do you want me to say? I already said we're just friends!" I burst out and all of them snorted. "We are!" I insisted and Daniella and Isadora exchanged knowing glances.

"Right, you do know how Strider asked me to marry him right?" Isadora started and both Daniella and Gwennie burst into laughter. I raised an eyebrow and Zach shot them confused looks.

Gwennie stopped laughing long enough to explain it to Zach. "Turns out that Isadora and my brother Strider were shagging buddies. And one day he just popped the question. Isa over here almost slapped him."

Zach chuckled under his breath and Daniella let out a delicate snort. "You should've seen how Cameron proposed. Everything went wrong that day. Our dinner reservations were cancelled, he lost the ring and to top it off he hit the waiter and as a result, guess who got soaked in beer."

All three females burst into more laughter and Zach joined in and shook his head with an amused laugh. "You Donnahue women."

Isadora straightened up. "See this just proves that you Donnahue men are no good at courting women. Even Emmett I'm sure. So why are you and this Emma 'just friends'?" She questioned and sipped from her tea.

I glared at Isadora and answered sullenly. "I already told you before remember? When Gwennie announced her engagement to us."

"Wait what?" Daniella questioned confused and Gwennie shot both Isadora and I a scowl and hissed. "He told you but not me?!"

"Yes. He told me. Too bad for you bitches but long story short. She doesn't like that he's famous." Isadora smirked and crossed her arms over her chest with a smug expression on her face. Clearly happy that she was privy to information that others weren't.

Daniella raised an eyebrow at Isadora's announcement. "Huh, I thought he being famous would work in his favour. But I guess not."

Rolling my eyes at that, I scoffed and remained silent to see Zach giving me a lopsided grin. "Yeah. That's Emma."

"So Jack, how are you on wooing her? I assume that's what you've been doing. How old is Emma anyway? What's her full name?"

And that was how it began. The questions started pouring and I groaned inwardly. It felt like my mother was around again. Which I didn't know about considering she died when I was five, Gwennie was three and Emmett was about one.

I didn't have a good relationship with my mother. She was too busy playing the society hostess while my father was a distant one. Right now, he was off God knows where doing who knows what. It was clear that he wanted nothing to do with his children and grandchildren. And it was fine by me because no one really wanted him around anyway.

"I'm not wooing her. We're just friends and we hang out. I think she's twenty-six or twenty-seven. I'm not telling her full name. You people are going to hunt her down."

I finished and shifted in my seat from the three glares aimed my way. "Is that all you got to say?" Isadora scowled and the rest of the meeting went this way. With my sister and sister-in-laws probing and fishing for details and answers which I ignored or diverted to wedding plans for Gwennie and Zach.

However at times, I could see Zach studying me with a scrutinising expression as I refused to answer questions about Emma and I had been wondering when he was about to ask me about her.

It turned out that Zach had finally gotten his chance when Isadora and Daniella left and Gwennie was in the washroom. "So Jack, what are your actual intentions with Emma?"

I shoved my hands in the pockets of my jeans and shrugged awkwardly. "We're just friends." I offered and Zach snorted. "Right...."

He sighed and stared me right in the eye. "I've known Emma my whole life and all I can say is, if you hurt her, you'll have to deal with me." Zach says seriously and I nodded.

"I know. I wouldn't expect otherwise. And Emma and I are just friends. I'm sure she thinks that I'm less than a friend." I muttered the last part under my breath and Zach snorted and gave me a grin.

"You're alright Jack." He clapped a hand on my back and straightened as Gwennie made her way to us.

"Well, seeing that this meeting is absolutely fruitless. I'm leaving." My sister announced with a scowl and tugged Zach to follow after her.

All I could do was shake my head at my family members before I headed for a party at a fellow actor's house.

* * *

A/N: Hi guys, here is the next chapter and I hope you guys love it. Thanks so much for being patient and let me know your thoughts on this. Please vote and comment? Thank you guys for reading and I love you all so much! <3

Chapter 11-The Movie Marathon I

Chapter 11-The Movie Marathon I

Jack Donnahue's POV

I shifted around in my seat before taking steady breaths and hauled the bag of romantic comedy films out of the car and headed towards Emma's home.

It was our planned movie marathon and well we had agreed to take turns watching the different genre of movies. I was a little wary about that, Emma favoured movies that had the thriller genre and I knew that included horror movies. I wasn't scared of them, I just wasn't a fan.

But hey, if I watched those, Emma would have no choice but to watch the ones I brought. And I brought quite a few that I thought she may like.

Pulling my cap over my head more and adjusted my sunglasses, I knocked on the door before waiting. Emma only agreed to let me come over when

Ella was asleep which was about nine. Tapping my foot impatiently, the door finally opened and Emma sighed as she spotted the bag containing the rom-coms.

"You were serious weren't you?" She pressed her lips into a thin line and I gave her a lopsided grin. "Of course. I've got some that I think you would like." I took off my sunglasses and shoved them into the bag along with my cap.

Sighing heavily, Emma rolled her eyes before opening the door wider so that I could enter. "I was really hoping you would forget. But, I've got my favourites too." She shot me a sly grin and I swallowed harshly.

"Great. Let's start. Ella's asleep right?" I hastily questioned as I warily eyed the stack of horror films on the coffee table. Emma nodded her head and wandered into the kitchen and brought out a bowl of popcorn and some drinks before settling onto the couch. "Yeah she is."

I eyed her cautiously as she picked up a horror film and got ready to slide it into the DVD player. "Why don't we watch one of mine first to start?"

Emma shot me an amused glance and I expected her to start teasing me but she didn't. "Alright. Go ahead and pop it in." She gestured and inwardly, I breathed out a sigh of relief and slid the disk in.

"The Proposal?" Emma read the title out skeptically. "It's good." I flashed her a charming grin and she shrugged before tucking her feet under her as she pressed the play button. "If you say so." She muttered under her breath and ran her fingers through her hair.

"It is!" I insisted and soon the movie started playing. Sitting on the couch, my eyes studied Emma's house more carefully. It was pretty normal and sophisticated looking, the walls were painted in warm tones and the colour scheme was something that suited her personality.

However, evidence of a child living here was obvious due to some misplaced toys and crayons, along with children sized shoes. Emma's home was pretty large, I could see a dining room, along with five doors down the hallway and more above. Vaguely, I wondered about what her bedroom looked like.

Studying Emma from the corner of my eyes, I hadn't taken in her appearance yet and I realised she was dressed in black leggings and an oversized long sleeved shirt. Her dark hair was left as it is and fell down her shoulders. And the expression on her face as she watched the starting of the movie was one of slight curiously and skepticism.

Well, I was confident that she would enjoy it. How could anyone not like it? I grabbed some popcorn and chewed on it while studying her from the corner of my eyes. It was safe to say that throughout the entire movie, I was paying more attention towards the expressions on Emma's face than the movie itself.

In my defence, I had watched this film many times with Gwennie and with my sisters-in-law. Hence, I could say that I knew the film extremely well.

Throughout the movie, the expressions ranging across Emma's face was mostly frowns and confusion and narrowed gazes. She didn't even laugh at the funny parts while I, who have watched this film so many times, laughed. How could she not find it funny? I found it funny? I was speechless.

When the film finally ended, I turned to Emma and asked hopefully, "So? What do you think? It was good wasn't it?"

Emma turned to me, an adorable frown marring her face as she replied. "Well, I was right, it was as ridiculous as I thought it would be."

I groaned and dragged my hand over my face. "What? How could you not like it? It was funny as hell and probably the best I've ever seen!"

Emma raised an eyebrow and shot me a pointed look. "That probably explains a lot." Her eyes were glinting with humour at my appalled behaviour and I guessed she must have thought it was funny.

I glared at her and crossed my arms. "Just you wait! I'll find a film that is a rom-com that you would love! I swear it!" I was determined for that to happen and I didn't care how long it will take for that to happen.

"Right, well, now it's my choice of movie and I'm going with The Conjuring." Emma said dryly before giving me a sly smirk as she held up the DVD case.

I was royally fucked.

I could feel my face turning pale. I had heard about that movie. It was said to be one of the best horror films ever made and I had avoided it at all costs even when Emmett wanted to watch it.

"Yeah sure." I mumbled and quickly grabbed a can of coke before sipping at it as Emma got off the couch to slide the disc in. Great. I thought mournfully as I spotted the design of the DVD case. I wasn't scared of horror films, I just disliked them with a strong passion.

Not that I was going to tell Emma that of course.

However, despite my brain preparing me mentally for the torture I was going to go through, I couldn't help but admire the way Emma's legs looked liked in her black leggings. Her oversized long sleeved shirt had dropped to the right, baring her shoulder and I could see her black bra strap.

Quickly averting my eyes, I focused my attention on the table, noting the other horror films she had there. What the hell was wrong with her?

"Alright, it's starting." Emma announced, her hazel eyes lighting with mischief as she looked at me with anticipation. Why the hell was she staring at me like that? Oh. She probably thought I was going to scream like a little girl. Well, I would show her!

I, Jack Donnahue wasn't a chicken and I would get through this nonsense of a film without shrieking like a little girl. I thought determinedly and Emma let out a laugh before pressing the play button.

* * *

"HOLY FU-" I shouted and a slim dainty hand clasped over my mouth, cutting me off.

Emma shot me a tiny glare before jerking her head to the hallway. "Ella is asleep. Keep your voice down."

I nodded and when I realised that Emma's hand was still covering my mouth, I grinned and stucked my tongue out to lick her hand. Emma let out a little squeak in disgust.

"Oh god, Jack! What is wrong with you?" Emma gasped as she quickly stood up and headed to the kitchen. I burst into laughter and the sound of the tap running made me laugh even more.

The sudden scare from the movie faded and I relaxed slightly. Who the fuck invented horror films? Whoever did must be insane. How was getting scared considered a thing? And, why the hell wasn't Emma freaking out? I knew my sister was afraid of this sort of thing. Why wasn't Emma?

Emma entered the living room and took her place beside me. Her eyes were fixed on the screen before she shot me a smirk. "If I had known you were afraid of horror films, we could have watched a Disney one instead. Ella loves Frozen, you look like Hans."

I huffed and glared at her. "I certainly do not look like that lame ass pompous character in that show! And I wasn't afraid, it was just really. ..sudden."

Honestly, Emma was right - not that I was going to admit it - I was bloody freaking out. How the hell was she not fazed by any of this?! I was still screaming internally from the horror film. Jesus. What the fuck!

I placed a hand on my chest, willing my heart to calm down. And again, why was the living room so dark? I was still freaking out and the storm that was pouring right not was bloody not helping!

Without a doubt, I knew I wouldn't be getting any sleep tonight. Maybe, I could ask Emmett to drop by. Jesus, get a grip! I was twenty-nine years old, why the hell was I afraid of a horror film?

Especially when I was an actor and knew how all the effects and makeup made the movie. This was ridiculous. I was ridiculous. What the hell was wrong with me. The scream of the woman in the film made me wince and I shuddered as shivers went down my spine.

Hearing a laugh, I turned to Emma to see that she was smiling and laughing softly at the screen. What the fuck was wrong with her? Clearly, I was be-friending someone who was a closet psychopath. My brain was screaming at me as the movie continued.

And I had a strong suspicion that Emma knew that I was freaking out from the film. I wasn't a mind reader, but it was pretty obvious whenever I jumped or inhaled sharply whenever something horrible happened.

When the fucking movie - finally - ended, I was completely silent. My eyes were still on the television even though Emma had already removed the disk. "How was it?" She questioned, a smirk on her lips as she kept the disk in a drawer.

"Nghhhh." That was the only sound I could make. My heart was still racing and I was pretty sure I was traumatised.

Emma studied me, her smirk turning into a fully amused grin as she noted the state I was in. "Huh, now I know why you only act in romantic comedy or action films. You're obviously too afraid to act in horror films."

That brought me out of my dazed state and I glared up at her as she chewed on the remaining popcorn in the bowl. "No," I replied indignantly before continuing as I crossed my arms over my chest defensively. People who act in horror films are those with no talent. I have it that's why I'm in action or romantic films."

Emma raised an eyebrow at me but I could see that she was holding back a laugh. "Right...If you say so."

"It is so!" I insisted, "You don't see anyone famous doing horror films now do you?"

She shot me an unimpressed stare before crossing her arms. "Well no, but, I still think you're too chicken to do a horror film." I knew she was goading me and I was not going to fall for it.

I sniffed disdainfully and snorted. "No, they don't pay as much. Besides, I don't have time for that. And besides, can you imagine the headlines saying that I accepted a horror film? My career will vanish faster than one-hit wonders. Like that guy who sang that Uptown Trunk or something."

Emma bit back a laugh before commenting dryly, "You're such a snob. Anyway, I don't really think that you would be featured on the front page of any newspaper. Tabloids or magazines maybe."

"Why the hell not?" I questioned with a frown and Emma shook her head before sitting down. "You're just an actor Jack. And like I said, I don't really consider that as a profession."

I glared at her indignantly. "Take that back! It is counted as a job!"

Emma rolled her eyes. "Hardly-" Interrupting her, I lunged at her and dug my fingers at her sides. "I'll tickle you until you take it back!" I threatened.

"I'm not ticklish." She shot me a smug grin and I scowled down at her. "What?" Testing her announcement, I pressed my fingers at her sides and waited to hear her laughing hysterically but nothing.

"Are you serious?" I groaned exasperatedly. Honestly, this was the only way I could ever convince Gwennie to do something that she didn't want. Emma burst into quiet laughter and smirked. "Too bad, now get off me. You brought more films didn't you?"

I had not realised the position we were in. I was over her and Emma was lying down on the couch, her face was flushed from laughing at my expense and I was between her slim legs. Hoping that she wouldn't notice, I got off her casually and feigned weariness.

"Yes obviously, you wouldn't appreciate them. But I don't care, I'm determined to make you like them!" I announced and Emma scoffed before reaching out for her drink. "Bring it on."

"Oh, I will!" Emma laughed at my response and I grinned back at her, noting how gorgeous she looked.

* * *

A/N: Hi guys, I finally updated! Sorry for the long wait! I know that some of you were so impatient and afraid that this book was on hold or being discontinued. Well, its not. I've just been so busy with school and my other book but now that TOK has been finished, I can get back to updating this.

Anyway, I hope that you guys love this chapter! I had so much fun writing this and please show your support by voting and commenting? ;) Also, updates for this book is once every week? I really wish I could update faster but I'm in my second year of business school and its getting even more insane. Do bear with me! But if I can update faster, I would! But at least, I would update every week! I love you guys and thanks so much for reading!

Chapter 12-The Parents

Chapter 12-The Parents

Emmaline Heywood's POV

I stepped into the room quietly, my breath hitching as I caught sight of the still body of my twin. Biting on my lower lip, I moved closer to the hospital bed and looked down at Theo.

His brown hair had gotten longer and was now past his ears. A rueful smile crossed my face at that sight, my brother, being the vain human being he was would have freaked out at the current state of his hair.

Even though we were twins, neither Theo or I looked alike. We were fraternal twins after all. But the only thing we shared in common was our dark hair. He had lighter brown eyes and sharp cheekbones while my face was sightly rounder with softer features. The smile faded when I noticed that he looked slightly more gaunt than before.

I visited as often as I could, about once a week and it never failed to hit me emotionally at the sight of my twin in this state. Placing my bag onto the chair, I replaced the flowers in the vase with the new ones I had gotten earlier.

Even though I've thought about it plenty of times, I've never understood how my brother had turned to drugs and in a way, I blamed myself for not catching on to what he was doing. I was his twin! Shouldn't I have known? If I had caught on quicker, I would have been able to pull my brother out of his depressed state and maybe, I would have been able to prevent him from all of this.

Guilt still ate at me ever since Theo had fallen into a coma and I've felt as if I had failed him. The thought of my brother turning to drugs had never ever crossed my mind, it didn't fit into his character.

Theo had always been someone that was positive, cheerful, fun and he loved living and being an actor. Whereas, I was the one that was pessimistic and serious. In some way, we were opposites but we complemented each other.

I sunk down onto the chair and stared at his unmoving body, had it not been for the slight movement of his chair, I would've sworn he was dead.

"You're such an idiot," I muttered quietly. "What the hell were you thinking? Drugs?"

Silence filled the room and I pressed my lips together and once I've felt that my emotions were under control, I continued, "Ella got your way of talking me into things. Today, she convinced me to get her ice-cream before lunch and I gave in. Both of you are so alike."

"You would love her. She wonders about you, you know? And I don't have the heart to tell her that you're here in the hospital." I pause and sucked in a breath before reaching out to run my fingers through his long dark hair.

I glanced around the room, noting the bare walls and the almost empty room. "I managed to realise why she had gotten her way, she pulls that exact puppy dog face that you do."

As I studied his appearance, I noted the dark circles under his eyes, his sharp cheekbones and he was so pale that he was almost white. "Why didn't you ever tell me what you were going through?"

"You were there for me when I needed you. Why couldn't you have let me done the same? I would have helped, I would have done anything for you. We're twins aren't we?"

Anger and desperation laced my tone and I inhaled sharply to hold these emotions back. Often, I wondered why Theo hadn't come to me when he was suffering from depression and doing drugs? Had I done something to alienate him? Had I offended him in some way? It hurt that he wouldn't even come to me for help, after everything we had been through together.

We always had each other's backs. Our parents didn't care much for us. They were more involved and interested in getting richer and famous. I knew for a fact that they only visited Theo once according to the guest log in from the hospital.

I was the one paying for Theo's treatment and his stay here in the hospital, not that I minded but it was still a sore point that our parents couldn't be bothered in their child's health to contribute to his fees or even visit him.

As the one paying for his fees, I had made sure that Theo had gotten a private and secluded ward where no one would be able to disturb him and that included the reporters. Also, only a select number of people were given clearance to visit him.

I've never brought Ella to visit Theo once. It was a well known fact that Theo was in a coma and since he had been in the prime of his acting and modelling career, it was big news that he had been into drugs.

Somehow, the reporters had gotten news that Theo was in this exact hospital and as a result, I didn't dare to bring Ella along. I would never subject her to the kind of life I had when I was younger.

Seeing that today was a Friday and I was supposed to be working from home while Ella was off in kindergarten, I took the day to spend some time with Theo before fetching Ella.

Feeling a little hungry, I stood up along with my bag before heading down to the hospital cafeteria to get something to eat.

Once I was done, I quietly made my up back to Theo's ward, smiling politely at the nurses who recognised me. Due to patient confidentially, it wasn't leaked that I was Emmaline Grey Heywood and I was glad for that.

However once I entered Theo's room, I stopped and stared in horror and shock as I surveyed the various lights and cameraman in the room.

My eyes were wide and I pretty see I looked like a goldfish with how far my jaw dropped but I didn't care. The sight of my parents cooing over their son who was in a coma because of the cameras.

Rage filled my body and I could not believe the audacity they had. The fake concern that was bestowed onto Theo was practically oozing from them and I could feel it all the way at the door.

I guess my entrance must have gotten the cameraman's attention because the giant thing was swung into my direction and my mother started shrieking before clamouring towards me.

"Emmaline! I can't believe you're back!" My mother gushed before throwing her arms around me.

Meanwhile, my father remained beside Theo, false happiness appeared on his face as he stood there watching me.

Gritting my teeth, I took a step back, causing my mother's arms to drop to her side limply.

Ignoring her, I turned towards the cameraman and the rest of the crew and snarled, "Get out. All of you! Get out!"

One of the man, who I guessed was the director or something like that frowned and protested, "We're in the middle of shooting, we can't just leave."

I was one step closer to slapping him and I quickly reigned in my anger before barking out, "I don't care, stop filming and erase the tape this instant because neither I or my brother signed up to be part of this sort of ridiculous, useless charade! And if all of you don't get the hell out of here in thirty seconds, I will the cops and file for a lawsuit!"

The director glared at me before gesturing for everyone to leave. Everyone slowly shuffled out of the room with all the equipment leaving my fuming parents in the room. Honestly, which nurse or doctor allowed all this non-sense in the hospital? Especially in my brother's ward when I instructed only a select number of people to visit? Swearing to find out who was it, I turned to my mother with a dark scowl on my face.

"What are you still doing here? I told you to leave!"

Even though I hadn't seen my parents personally in nine years, they looked exactly the same. Eyeing my mother critically, I could see that she had her hair bleached again and had gone under the knife more than once.

Adeline Heywood was in her fifties but she looked like she was twenty years younger. Her skin looked tight and stiff and I was pretty sure she had her nose done more than once. Also, she looked even skinnier than me, it was safe to say, that my mother was the typical Hollywood starlet who loved to be in the limelight. Turning to my father, I could tell that he was wearing a wig and he also had gone through at least some plastic surgery.

My mother glared at me and crossed her arms, "Why on earth did you do that Emmaline? It was perfect! A family reunion coming together for the sake of my son who is your brother who is in a coma!"

I. Could. Not. Fucking. Believe. It.

Clenching my fists, I straightened my posture and stared down at her condescendingly, "It never fails to bring me into a state of disbelief that you care more about television ratings than your own son."

I narrowed my stare at her before shifting it towards my father, "Don't you care that your only son was depressed and had turned to drugs and now is in a coma that he may never wake from?"

My mother sniffed, showing her true colours now that the cameras were gone. "He'll be fine. It's just a coma. It's no big deal. Now, I'm going to invite the cameras back. Ratings will increase and could you act like you're all pleased to see us-"

My stare grew colder and seeing that I towered over her, I sneered down at her frostily. "I thought we weren't family since I was seventeen. That was nine years ago."

My mother waved her hand dismissively. "Whatever, your father and I need something fantastic to boost the ratings! You coming back would increase it!"

"No."

"But-"

"Get the hell out!" I gritted my teeth and pointed to the door.

Due to my response, my father entered the conversation, his brown eyes flashing fiercely at me, "You would think that our own daughter could be any less selfish than she was. After all, we supported you during the accident."

With that very statement, I lost it.

"I'm the one that is selfish?" I started disbelievingly before raising my voice. "Who exactly is the one who is more concerned about stupid television ratings than their own son who could never wake up! Theo is your own flesh and blood and yet you're not even concerned about him, neither are you paying his bills! Your son could be dead and you wouldn't even care!"

My mother stiffened and glared back at me defensively, "Of course we would care-"

I cut her off, not even halfway finished as I brushed past her and went towards my father. "Regarding the accident, you have no idea what the hell you are talking about! You and mother were never supportive! You acted as if everything was something to be splashed across television! The people who really supported me during that year was Theo and Zach! Not you or mother!"

I took a deep breath before levelling the coldest and hateful stare I could give and spoke lowly, "So don't you ever dare accuse me of that ever again! Now get the hell out. I don't want to see you ever again!"

My father shot me a resentful glare before dragging my mother out of the room.

When the room was quiet once more, I sunk down onto the chair and shut my eyes, bracing my body over the bed and covered my face with my hands as I tried to push back all the emotions my parents wrought out of me.

It was funny to think that even nine years had passed since I last saw them, they still could affect me in that manner. And I hated that they could.

Pushing all those memories and emotions that had happened oh so long ago, I shuddered and took another deep breath, willing myself to calm down before I picked Ella up. Somehow, she could always tell if something was troubling or worrying me. Obviously, I didn't want her to pick up on my inner turmoil.

Glancing at my watch, I could see that it was time to leave and I stood up and gave Theo one last lingering glance before leaving. Of course, I instructed the nurse to move Theo into another room and ward and removed my parents' name off the list that allowed them to visit him.

Initially, I had thought they cared enough, but after today? It was clear that they couldn't care less. It shouldn't sting seeing that I knew what kind of people they were but nonetheless, it still did.

Strengthening my resolve to ignore whatever happened today, I shouldered my bag and walked back to the car and picked Ella up from kindergarten.

The car was filled with joyful chatter and giggling as Ella talked about her day and as I looked at the

five year old, I was more than determined to keep her away from my parents and to give her the best normal childhood I could.

After all, it was something I never had.

* * *

A/N: Hi guys! Here is the update as promised and it's finally a little reveal about Emma and her family. I know you guys will be: That's it? Yes, that's all you're getting for now! Sorry about the absence of Jack in this chapter, he would appear in the next one ;)

Anyway, I hoped that you liked this chapter and please vote and comment! Love you all so much and thanks so much for reading! <3

Chapter 13-The Scheme

Chapter 13- The Scheme

Emmaline Heywood's POV

I frowned as I flipped through the files regarding the Greek artefacts that would be arriving next week for the Greek exhibition that would be happening in about four months time.

It turns out that the shipment would be late by about a week. That wasn't good considering the fact that the opening of the exhibition would have to be delayed as well. Drumming my fingers on my desk, I contemplated between requesting for more workers to set up the exhibition or delay the opening by a week.

The door opened and Zach strolled in, a pair of sunglasses shielding his eyes while sipping on a cup of iced coffee. Immediately, my mind went towards Jack.

This wasn't the first time that happened of course. The simple sight of Zach wearing a pair of sunglasses brought up the memory of Jack wearing them.

Coffee even reminded me of him.

I was definitely going mad. I quirked up an eyebrow at Zach who slid into the chair opposite mine and slid a cup of coffee that I had not notice was in his hand.

"Here, I got that thing you like. The butterscotch one which is strange because I have to ask, since when the hell did you like coffee?"

I avoided his gaze and stared at the cup containing the butterscotch flavoured coffee. Yes. That. The coffee. The same kind that Jack had gotten for me those few weeks ago.

Of course I blamed my sudden fondness for coffee on Jack. It was he that had influenced me to like them. Not that I was going to tell Zach that, he would certainly have a field day if he knew.

"I thought it was interesting that there was a butterscotch flavour for coffee. And you know I love anything to do with butterscotch." I replied, my gaze still firmly on my desk as I nonchalantly fiddled with the stationary.

Tweaking all my pens to the right, I looked up to see Zach eyeing me warily. "Is everything alright? You have that look on your face when you met someone unpleasant."

"Is it one of those nosy teachers wondering who Ella's parents are?" Zach pressed and I shook my head. "No, my parents. I met them at the hospital on Friday."

Immediately, Zach cursed and I quickly took a sip of the coffee as my best friend let out more strings of expletives that would have made my pretentious father proud. "What the fuck happened?" He demanded as a scowl crossed his face.

Ever since we had been friends, Zach had hated my parents just after the first five minutes of meeting them and well, it was safe to say that my parents disliked him in return. They felt that he wasn't good enough to be friends with, seeing that he was a nobody in Hollywood.

"Harsh words were exchanged. What else did you expect? Those nine years clearly didn't have any difference on them." I answered tonelessly, disguising the bitterness and resentment I had for my own parents.

Zach sighed heavily and reached for my hand. "Well, you don't need them anyway, you have me and Theo, and now Ella. You know I'll always be here for you."

I forced a tight smile on my face, not wanting to talk about my parents or anything or anyone from my childhood. "Yeah I know. Thank you. Anyway, what brings you by?"

Zach wrinkled his nose and slumped into the chair and sighed dramatically, "Gwennie and I went for cake testing and I guess she got sick of my whining and she told me to get lost while she made a decision."

A small smile crossed my face at that. "What's there to complain about? You love cake."

"Yeah, I know that," Zach huffed but continued, "until I realised that Gwennie only wanted flavours that were exotic, and that didn't include chocolate. It also doesn't help when I only get small bite sized pieces!"

At that, I couldn't help but laugh a little. "Thats the point of cake testing idiot."

Zach rolled his eyes in response and muttered. "Whatever. Anyway, thats why I'm here. To bother you until Gwennie is done with god knows what."

I let out a small smile at that and as I studied my best friend who I remembered as the comic book fanatic when we were young was getting married in a few scant months. "Speaking about Gwendolyn, I've never really met her."

Zach stared at me before offering me a sheepish grin. "I know, but I've been trying to put off the inevitable." At my questioning expression, Zach continued, "You are either going to like her or you're going to hate her."

I raised an eyebrow at that before shooting him a skeptical glance, "What?"

"Yes its true, I'm marrying an anal, uptight, bossy, nosey, direct woman and I love her." Zach flashed me a grin and I laughed and shook my head disapprovingly. "Honestly, you shouldn't say that about your fiancée. She might hear you."

Waving his hand dismissively, Zach slouched, "Nah, she can't."

"I can and I'm not anal nor am I uptight!"

Both Zach and I swung our eyes towards the door and there stood a short dark haired woman who was shooting glares at my best friend. From Zach's unrepentant grin, I could safely say that I would be meeting his fiancée.

I eyed the dark haired woman and watched with mild amusement as she stalked towards Zach and swatted his shoulder before giving me her attention. "You must be Emma, I'm Gwendolyn Donnahue, Zach's fiancée." She took out a hand for me to shake and I shook her hand.

"Its nice to finally meet you." I said evenly as I made sure I kept my expression neutral. Of course I knew that Zach was marrying Jack's sister but the reality of that was hitting home right now.

She was pretty and had the same arrogant features that Jack had. However, his features were more relaxed and welcoming while Gwendolyn's was colder and more sharp. But, it was clear that they were siblings, both shared the same hair and eye colour. To be very honest, I had not expected Zach to marry someone who was his total opposite.

I could feel Gwendolyn eyeing me critically before she finally spoke. "I'm sure you've met my brother Jack. He talks about you a lot."

At that, I raised an eyebrow and I could feel Zach trying to stifle his laughter. Honestly, where was the best friend loyalty? "I didn't expect that from him." I replied coolly, not wanting to give anything away.

Inwardly, a brief panic flashed through me at the thought of her recognising me. After all, I had been a model and in reality tv shows when I was younger. But after a few more moments of her scrutinising me, Gwendolyn eased her stare before breaking into a more relaxed state.

"I don't see why you're still hanging around my brother. He's hopeless," Gwendolyn said as she stepped closer towards the desk and looked around my office. "I hope you would forgive for simply barging in. The receptionist told me to enter when I asked for you."

I am going to kill Roxanne. What exactly was the point of having a receptionist if she was going to direct everyone here. First, Jack, now his sister. Who was going to be next?

"It's fine. After all, its good to finally meet you in person. Zach doesn't excel well in social etiquette." I offered and shot my best friend a pointed glance who was watching our exchange with wide innocent eyes.

"Hey!"

Gwendolyn cracked a smile at that and her eyes landed on my desk as if she was searching for something before her eyes met my face once more. "I would have to agree with that. I hope you would excuse me, I have a lunch appointment to get to. It was very nice meeting you."

I offered a tight smile as I noticed her eyes glancing around the room again. "Like wise."

Gwendolyn smiled at me before leaving. Zach stood up to go after her but turned to me and grinned. "She thinks you're okay. This went better than I thought."

"What?" Zach nodded and shoved his hands into his pockets. "She wasn't shooting you glares and giving judgemental glances. You're alright in her books."

I shrugged and sat back down in my chair, "That's good to know. Don't you have to get going?" Zach laughed before sauntering out of the room. Shaking my head and trying to calm down the slight panic that Zach's fiancée had given me, I turned back to my files.

* * *

"I met her!" Gwendolyn announced with barely suppressed glee as she strode towards the table where her sister-in-laws were waiting impatiently.

Isadora and Daniella's attention snapped towards Gwendolyn as she sat down, a smug smirk on her face. "What? Who? You don't mean Jack's mystery girl!"

"Exactly. I met her earlier. And for once, I'm way ahead of both of you. Suck it bitches."

Isadora huffed and tossed her dark hair behind her shoulders before crossing her arms over her chest. "Whatever! Details now!"

Gwendolyn settled into her chair, the smug grin never leaving her face. "She's so different from Jack's usual girls. I mean I could hardly get a read from her. And she seemed way too smart for Jack, I mean hell, she works in a museum."

Danielle raised an eyebrow before tucking an auburn curl behind her ear. "You can't get a read from her? You're always very good at reading people."

Isadora leant forward, interest gleaming in her eyes. "No, I can't. It's like she's holding herself back. You can tell she's very reserved. Nonetheless, I think she's perfect for Jack." Gwendolyn pursed her lips, deep in thought.

In her opinion, Gwendolyn could see that Emma was very cautious and quiet, but if push came to shove, Emma would strike silently. She was pretty but very reserved and while she was in her office, Gwendolyn couldn't spot one single picture of anyone or any personal items.

"How the fuck is that going to happen? From the way you described her, she sounds extremely difficult and stubborn." Isadora frowned as she drummed her fingers on the table.

Gwendolyn smirked and shot her a condescending stare. "She sounds like you, the difficult and stubborn part."

Isadora scoffed and crossed her arms over her chest before sneering. "If that's true, you're a spoilt little bitch!"

Daniella sighed as both of them started to bicker - again - and she ignored them. They had more pressing things to discuss, such as Jack's love life, or well, the lack of it. But how on earth were they going to set this up?

Her sister-in-law had described Emma as someone who was extremely smart and hence would be able to detect a hint of any matchmaking from a kilometre away.

"I dare you to say that again! I fucking dare you!"

"Pipe it down Gwennie, any louder, you might have to write your vows out to Zach during the ceremony."

Well, Daniella wasn't a saint and she certainly couldn't help but burst into laughter at Isadora's comment and in return, received a frosty glare from her sister-in-law. Suddenly, she was struck with an idea. No, it was the idea. The idea that would work. The idea that would bring Emma and Jack together!

"We could ask her to help plan the wedding! And if she asks, we can say we want her input as Zach is her best friend!"

Daniella announced before smirking smugly at the other two women who stopped arguing long enough to ponder on her suggestion. Isadora nodded her head approvingly, "Hmm, yes. You are onto something! It'll work. And all of us would be able to meet her!" Isadora crowed and Gwendolyn made a face.

"Would that really work? Maybe we could ask her for lunch and stuff and Jack would pop by coincidentally." Gwendolyn said thoughtfully, her eyes starting to gleam with mischief and excitement.

"Yes, it would. I can't wait to see Jack bumbling about like an eager school-boy!" Isadora cackled and the three women began discussing and plotting.

* * *

Hi, guy! Here is the update! By the way, let me know what you guys think. And please vote and comment! Also! What do you guys think about the other writing style I experimented in? Love you all and thanks so much for reading!

Chapter 14-The Lunch

Chapter 14-The Lunch

Jack Donnahue's POV

"I don't see why I have to go." I grumbled as I followed behind Gwennie who was ahead of me as she ignored my complaints.

"I just had lunch with you three witches from hell just last week," I made a face and continued, "The only difference is that Zach is going to be there."

Gwennie let out a huff and turned around before jabbing her index finger into my chest as she snapped. "One more word Jack, you won't see a witch, but a demon from hell!"

With that, she turned around and strode into a cafe that Daniella liked to frequent. Scowling, I glared at her head from the back as I followed her. It wasn't as if she could see me but it made me feel better.

Behind me, Max lumbered along, trying not to laugh as he maintained a professional image but I knew that deep down, he was laughing at the fact that my younger sister was bossing me around.

Not that it was unusual or anything, Gwennie had been bossing me around since the day she was born. Welcome to the life of being an older brother.

Entering the little cafe, I was pleased to note that Gwennie was walking towards a secluded corner where I already could see the other two-thirds of the women from the Donnahue family along with Zach who was conversing with Isadora who threw her head back and laughed.

However, it was the sight of the other occupant at that table that made me stop, causing Max to bump into me which in turn made me stumble and trip on the leg of a chair.

"Jack, you're such a klutz!" Gwennie hissed as she tugged me along to the table where I could feel embarrassment seep into my skin at Emma's amused stare.

"Emma, what are you doing here?" I questioned as panic rose and I tried to act blasé as I sat down opposite of her. She was seated at the extreme right while Zach was in between her and Daniella while Max was seated between Gwennie and and I and Isadora was at the head of the table.

"She's Zach's best friend and I thought it was about time we finally get to know her seeing that she's like his sister." Isadora cut in and as I stared at her, I could see a glint in her eyes.

Bloody fucking hell.

What the hell was Gwennie and my sisters-in-law up to? They really were the three witches from hell. "Hi Jack." she greeted and I offered her a charming grin and I couldn't help but notice that her hair was all down and she was dressed casually, far from the office clothing I often saw her in. But she still looked gorgeous. I could feel my mouth going dry just because she was there.

"I forgot to say hey." I offered lamely and I already could see all the female members of my family snicker under their breaths. I already knew Max was sniggering out loud and I could feel my ears heat up from embarrassment.

So fucking smooth Jack. Way to go you idiot!

"I see." Emma replied evenly, I could tell she was uncomfortable around my family members. Who wouldn't be? My family was full of obnoxious pushy nosey people who loved to stick their noses in other people's business. Mainly mine for example. Like right now.

Immediately, I glared at Daniella who got the hint and began bringing the attention to Gwennie's upcoming wedding. Satisfied that Isadora and Gwennie began arguing while Zach began placating an irate Gwennie.

Glad that the attention was off Emma and I and that Daniella was the most pleasant female in my family, I turned to Emma and gave her a charming grin. I knew that my family knew about Emma now and I didn't care that they were trying to help, I appreciated it but I didn't want them around when I tried to win Emma over.

Clearing my throat, I shot a glare to my family members that - thankfully - went unnoticed by both Emma and them, I started. "So when do you want to have our next movie marathon?"

Emma raised an eyebrow as she sipped from her tea carefully. "Next movie marathon? Don't tell me you have overcome your fear of horror movies."

I grimaced and leaned back in my chair as I crossed my arms over my chest defensively. "I wasn't scared."

"When you shriek, you sound like a girl." Emma pointed out with an amused grin on her face.

The very sight of that grin on her face sent a shock of longing in me and I wanted her to be mine. She was so different from the other girls I knew and met. But obviously, she didn't feel the same way. I couldn't read her well, with the others, I could always tell what they wanted from me but Emma?

She was like a safe that I didn't have the key too. Suddenly realising that I had to answer quickly, I shot her a scowl and retorted "I do not. I told you, I was shocked by the sudden jump scare! I told you that last time."

A smirk tugged on the corner of her mouth before she shot me a wry grin, "We would agree to disagree. So I assume you have a found better movies than the previous ones you brought over?"

Shrugging and tossing her a satisfied grin, "Obviously. I swore I would continue to find one that you liked no matter how long it will take."

Emma broke into a small smile before she shook her head and tucked a curl behind her ear. "Alright. But as usual, I get to choose the horror movies."

I fought back the urge to swallow harshly from the very thought of those films but I managed. I was not giving Emma anymore reason for her to make fun of me.

"Oh, Jack you didn't tell me you went to Emma's house. What did you do?" Isadora questioned loudly and a muscle under my eye twitched.

She is pregnant with your future nephew, don't reach out to strangle her. Strider would be extremely unhappy with you if you did that. I chanted in my head.

I offered a bland smile before answering. "Oh Emma doesn't like films that are in the romance and comedy genre. She finds it boring and ridiculous."

Already, I could see the three witches from hell start to snicker under their breaths. No doubt they were finding it funny that I always acted in films with genres that Emma disliked.

I really hated them at times. Sometimes, I just wished that Gwennie was five again and I could lock her in my old closet. I used to do that until she set fire to my bed.

"But Emma, Jack likes to act in those films, have you watched any of his?" This time, Daniella questioned with intrigue in her green eyes.

Alright, I changed my mind, Daniella was not helping. Why couldn't they leave Emma and I alone? That was all I wanted right this moment! Honestly, couldn't I get a break?

Catching a quick glance at Emma, I could see her cheeks heating up a little. With her hair down in messy curls, big hazel eyes and her pale cheeks with hints of pink, the very sight of her this way made her look all the more endearing to me.

"Actually, I've never seen any of his films, I prefer horror or thriller films." Emma replied, her gaze avoiding mine and somehow, I knew she was lying. A lopsided grin formed on my face and I knew that she must have had watched one of my films recently.

Good God, I felt like an idiot and I was pretty sure I had a silly grin on my face from that realisation.

"Really? Hmm, well, I could say the same. I've never watched any of Jack's films, I thought it was a little odd seeing that I knew him well especially all his bad habits like when he-"

My eyes widened and I cleared my throat loudly before hastily cutting in, "Anyway," I paused and shot a venomous glare to Daniella who hid a smirk as she sipped from her glass of whatever fizzy drink she had before continuing. "I doubt Emma needs to hear about that. Besides, Emma loves horror shows-"

"Oh really? You know Jack hates those right, I remember him running from the film screaming when we watched one." Gwennie cut in and I guessed her spat with Isadora was done.

"I was ten!" I shouted defensively. Could my family members stop making me out as if I was a wimp? Max had an expression on his face that seemed almost constipated from how much laughter he was holding in while Zach seemed to look highly amused by everything that was going on.

A small smile quirked up on Emma's face as she digested that tiny tidbit about me. I really was going to stuff Gwennie in my closet when I had the chance.

The rest of the lunch passed in the same fashion, my family members feeding Emma awful childhood stories, horrible anecdotes and god knows what and I was mortified while Zach and Max mostly stayed silent, watching the exchanges with amusement shining out of their eyes.

When Emma made her leave, I eagerly jumped at the opportunity to be alone with her and to avoid my family members and joined her and we walked out of the little restaurant with her. Seeing that I brought my fake beard and sunglasses, I was thankful that Max need not follow me about.

While leaving, I was a hundred percent sure that those witches were sniggering at me. They seriously weren't making it a secret from how loud they were.

We started strolling down the streets and the silence was comfortable but I didn't want silence, now that I was finally alone with Emma, I wanted to start a conversation but what?

"I'm sorry about my family members. I told you about them being obnoxious and pushy." I offered and shoved my hands in my pockets.

Emma offered me an amused glance as she shrugged, "They were really funny."

"Is your family like mine?" I blurted out and immediately, I wanted to take those words back. Shite. The subject of Emma's family was a touchy one and I went there. Fuck, what was I thinking?

Stupid, stupid, stupid.

"No. They aren't."

I swallowed at the awkward silence that filled up around us and once again, I was cursing myself for being an idiot. However, my curiosity rose. What exactly happened that made Emma refuse to talk about her family? Whatever it was, I wasn't going to push it. I struggled to think of something to say that would change the subject and said the first thing that came to mind.

"You look very pretty today." I blurted out. I hoped that she knew what I was trying to say. It wasn't a lie. In fact, it was the opposite of one. She was bloody gorgeous and the fact that she didn't seem to care about that made her all the more attractive to me.

Emma shot me a confused glance before turning her attention back to the streets. "Thank you."

"What about me? Don't I look handsome?" I pressed, not wanting conversation to stop.

Emma shook her head disapprovingly but I could see that she was fighting back a smile. "Yes. You look as handsome as Santa Claus because of that beard."

Scoffing, I shot her a glare. "Santa Claus? Take that back Em. I'm Jack Donnahue. I'm literally the definition of good-looking." I announced arrogantly and Emma shot me a flat look before rolling her eyes but I could see a twitch on her face.

"I can actually see the size of your head swelling up and I doubt you could even enter your own house due to the size of your ego." She commented dryly as she shoved her hands into the pockets of her jeans. The sun shining down on us was making her dark hair seem even lighter, highlighting the different tones present and I swallowed harshly.

But as her comment registered in my brain, I threw my head back and burst out laughing, God, where did Emma come up with all her descriptions? Suddenly, from the corner of my eye, I spotted a speeding cyclist heading our way from the back and without thinking, I threw an arm around Emma's shoulder and pulled her closer towards me just as the cyclist sped past.

Emma let out a squeak as her face landed in my chest and the scent of her hair reached my nostrils and I eagerly inhaled the sweet floral scent of her. The scent teased my nose and already, I knew that this very scent would remind me of her.

Realising the cyclist was long gone, I stepped back sightly to see if Emma was injured in any way. Looking down, I could see a hint of a blush rising on her pale cheeks and she offered me a tiny smile, "Thank you. I didn't notice the man speeding."

The very mention of the irresponsible cyclist sparked up annoyance and I frowned irritatedly, "Honestly, what the hell was that idiot thinking? This is a bloody pedestrian walkway, not some racing pavement for bicycles. He didn't even have the courtesy to alert us that he was coming. The guy's a menace, what if I didn't pull you away in time? What if he hit someone? Or even a kid like Ella's age-"

I was ranting away and I didn't even know that Emma had been watching me with a growing smile on her face and I cut myself off when I realised that. "What?" I demanded in a panic. Was there something on my face? Or was something wrong with my appearance? Did I do something wrong? Oh hell.

Emma shook her head at that very movement also made me realise that my arm was still around her shoulders. "Nothing. I just wanted to say thank you for moving me out of the way." She offered me a beautiful smile and right then and there, I could safely say that my heart flipped in my chest.

With that we continued walking and I was wondering if she realised that my arm was still over her shoulders as we walked or if she chose to ignore it. I certainly wasn't going to move my arm away unless she made a move to do so. But I had to admit that it felt...nice. Emma was of the perfect height that my arm lay on her shoulders without being too high or too low.

It felt effortless.

And maybe, just maybe, it was simply my imagination that Emma was pressing closer to my side.

After all, a man can dream, can't he?

* * *

A/N: Hi guys! Hope that you liked this chapter and I promise that the pace of the story will be progressing a lot quicker in the next chapter! Thanks for reading and please vote and comment! <3

Chapter 15-The Movie Marathon II

Chapter 15-The Movie Marathon II

Emmaline Heywood's POV

"Alright, I've got a good one! Here." Jack announced with a triumphant grin on his face as he handed me a DVD case. I eyed it skeptically before taking it from his hand.

My fingers brushing against his made a spark of awareness shoot through me and I barely suppressed a shiver from that very feeling. "Crazy, Stupid, Love?" I read out the title and frowned a little, "Well, it does sound crazy and stupid."

"Take that back!" Jack tossed one of my throw pillows in my face and I blinked before shooting him an unimpressed glare.

"Clearly not, after that. How old are you?" I scoffed and slid the disc into the player.

Jack shot me another charming grin and my heart rate sped up at that sight. God, I had it bad. Which was not a good thing. I had to get over this feeling of affection for him. Ugh. What was wrong of me? I was half-tempted to slam the back of my head against the wall to knock some sense into me but I forced myself not to.

"Like I said before, six-years-old. Hey! Ella and I can be besties!"

A grin tugged onto the corner of my mouth at that and I shook my head while Jack gave a lopsided grin. "Alright! Let's start! I can guarantee that you will love this one!"

I raised an eyebrow at that before reaching out for the remote to press the play button. The opening credits played and a bowl of popcorn almost hit my face due to Jack thrusting it into my direction and I took it grudgingly before settling back onto the sofa. Somehow, I noted that we were sitting impossibly close - closer than before but I made no effort to move away.

I could at least afford that little yearning to be near him even though I knew it was ridiculous.

Shifting about to get a comfortable spot, I eyed the stack of DVDs with the horror genre longingly. Those were my comfort zones. Not this sort of movies that had romance and god knows what. But I swear that if Jack thought it would be funny to bring that godawful movie Fifty Shades of Grey, he would definitely knew what a demon from hell behaved like.

That day when I had lunch with Jack and his family, he had confided in me about his annoyance with the three witches or demons from hell. Of course, that term was to refer to his sister and sisters-in-law.

Seeing how close they all were, even the relationships Jack had with Isadora and Daniella ache. It wasn't fair that I had gotten an awful family. I only knew that I had been observing the Donnahue family members that were present with longing and bitterness.

I would do anything to have family members that would annoy me with their little playful arguments and banters rather than have those that didn't give any shit about you. The only living relative who truly cared about me was in a coma and I had no idea if Theo would even wake.

Feeling melancholic, I pressed my lips together and quickly focused my attention back to the screen. Thinking of my family always made the mood sombre.

To be honest, I was barely paying attention to the movie, I thought it was a little ridiculous but fifteen minutes into the movie, I was paying more attention to Jack than to the film as he mouthed certain lines from the film. He was so engrossed in the movie platinum that I didn't realise that his left arm was wrapped around my shoulders and his hand was playing with a lock of my hair unconsciously.

This almost felt like a...date.

Not that I hoping this was a date or anything like that.

Chewing my lip, I shifted a little closer to him and the scent of him drifted towards me and his scent made me sigh inwardly. The cologne that he was wearing made my head spin and coupled with his own scent, I felt like a schoolgirl crushing madly on her favourite singer. Which in my opinion, was ridiculous. I was twenty-six years old, not some silly fourteen year old.

His scent was clean, a something with a hint of citrus accompanied with a spicy twist. It was addicting and when Jack had pulled me closer to him due to the speeding cyclist, I was ashamed to admit that I had pressed my nose into his shirt, inhaling this very scent.

It was a good thing that he had stepped away before realising I was inhaling his shirt. That would have been something quite difficult to explain.

The rest of the film passed in a blur and even though I was barely paying attention, I came to the very same conclusion that I started out with.

"So? How was it? It was good wasn't it?" Jack questioned brightly, his eyes sparkling with excitement and I couldn't help but let an amused wry smile cross my face at his enthusiasm.

"Sorry to disappoint you, no, I thought it was a little...out there."

"What?!"

A snort escaped me at the stunned and annoyed expression on Jack's face. Moving away from him to slide a horror film disc in this time, I was about to do so until Jack smacked my hands away and quickly inserted another disc into the player before I could react.

However, I did note that the disc was another that belonged to Jack.

"Hey! It's my turn to choose." I protested and shot him an annoyed stare and reached out to the disc player when a hand tugged onto the back of my shirt. "Nah, too bad. Finders keepers, losers weepers."

I gave him a flat stare, "That does not even apply to our situation!"

Jack smirked at me triumphantly and pulled me down back onto the sofa before shrugging. "Whatever, just sit down and watch. Like I said, I'm determined to make sure you like one of these rom-coms."

I sighed heavily and gave in reluctantly. I had a feeling Jack wouldn't let this matter go until I admitted defeat. I was half-tempted to simply take back my dislike for the earlier film so that Jack would forget about this and I would have but my pride was at stake!

Deciding to suffer through approximately two hours of romantic cheesiness and boredom, I leaned back onto the sofa with a slight scowl on my face.

"Lighten up Emma! Don't be such a stick in the mud! You'll like this one! I guarantee it!"

I gave the film playing on the television an irritated glare and muttered under my breath. "That was what you said about the earlier film."

Of course, Jack being Jack either chose to ignore me or didn't hear it. The movie began playing and I watched with slight disgust as the male character gave the female characters flowers. How unoriginal.

That led to a big hug and a kiss on the cheek with a candlelight dinner between the characters. Good god, this was becoming extremely ridiculous and cheesy. I was literally cringing from the whole thing.

"You know what I think? I think you've never been properly romanced!" Jack announced out of the blue and I turned to him with my brows raised.

"What?"

"Come on, admit it!" He grinned and shot me a lazy smirk in my direction.

I shot him a flat stare in return. "And what exactly do I have to admit?"

"That you've never been properly romanced." He grinned charmingly and I scoffed before looking back at the screen unimpressed. "I have."

"Really? With a proper kiss?" He smirked and I narrowed my eyes and stated, bored. "Yes. Of course." Jack grinned and wiggled his eyebrows. "Was it with tongue?"

I shot him a deadpanned expression, choosing not to reply and Jack laughed. Silence reigned as we turned our attention back to the film playing on the television. Suddenly, a rough calloused hand cupped my cheek and I could feel my body freeze in shock from that action.

Slowly, Jack turned my head towards his and my eyes met his. Inhaling sharply from the the intensity of his gaze, I could barely string together a sentence right this moment. His brown eyes were burning into mine and they were soft as he looked at me as he caressed my cheek gently with his thumb. That very action sent heat flaring up in me and I couldn't seem to tear my eyes away from his.

"Did he touch you like this?" He questioned, his voice soft but it seemed to echo around my living room and I could feel was the roughness of his hand on my cheek and it stunned me into speechlessness. In all the months I've known Jack, I had never seen him this serious before. There was no sign of laughter, no sign of humour and the teasing expression on his face was gone.

They were replaced with a serious version of the Jack I knew. His warm brown eyes were locked onto mine but I noted that those brown orbs glanced down at my lips occasionally.

Was this really happening?

Jack watched me and continued, his gaze never leaving my face as he leaned in slowly as if giving me the chance to pull away. "Did he lean in just before he kissed you?"

My breath hitched when his face neared mine and my grip on my shirt tightened. Right now, his face was mere millimetres away from mine and his scent - that I found so addicting - was more intense and it made my head spin.

Briefly, I wondered if he would taste the same as he smelled. My fingers itched to run themselves through his dark hair, wondering if they were as soft as they looked.

My breathing was erratic as hell when his lips almost brushed against mine and all I could do was stare at him transfixed before parting my lips involuntarily. Jack took it as an invitation and leaned even closer for our lips to meet.

However, I guessed he must have misjudged the angle for his lips to press against mine as our noses bumped against each other. A small laugh escaped me and Jack shot me a cheeky grin before managing to press his lips against mine tentatively.

His hand cupped my cheek and our lips pressed together slowly as if testing the kiss out. Jack's lips were a little chapped but soft, they were full and met mine perfectly well.

All I could think of was why the hell was I not protesting or pushing him away?

The answer was simple. I didn't care. I was sick of fighting my attraction to him and I couldn't be bothered anymore. I wanted him. I had spent hours wondering what it would be like kissing him, what it would be like to be his and him to me. All thought of protecting my identity and Ella's was flung out of the window. For once after the incident, I was being impulsive.

I knew I would regret it later but for now? It didn't matter. Thinking was overrated. Why bother thinking when there was an attractive male kissing you?

Throwing all caution to the wind and removing any thoughts from my head, I shut my eyes and gave in. I shifted my body so that it faced Jack and my hands crept up to his chest tentatively, enjoying the way his muscles tensed at my touch. Maybe I ought to take back what I said about seeing him without a shirt would cause me to sanitise my eyes.

The arm that was wrapped around my neck crept down my body and his fingers gripped onto my waist tightly. The other hand that was on my cheek moved down to my waist as well. Slowly, my hands drifted up to his neck and I wrapped them around his neck, enjoying the feel of the curls on the nape of his neck.

Seeing that I wasn't pushing him away, Jack pulled me closer towards him and deepened the kiss. The kiss went from slow and gentle to being a little more demanding and deliciously rough. I wasn't even aware that he had lifted me from the sofa and onto his thighs that I realised I was straddling him.

One of his hands left my waist and moved upwards to tangle itself in my mass of dark hair. We were chest to chest and his magnetising scent filled my brain. It felt like I was drugged. Drugged from Jack Donnahue's kisses and touch. All I knew was; Jack could really kiss.

His mouth moved eagerly against mine, his teeth nipping against my lower lip as his tongue explored every crevice and dip in my mouth. My hands had moved to his hair tangling my fingers with his soft brown locks and his hands was rubbing the exposed skin on my waist where my shirt had ridden up.

The kiss was turning hot and heavy and from the position I was in - I was straddling him, I could tell exactly how hot and heavy our kiss had been. I was pretty sure we would have been heading further had it not been for the loud gunshot that sounded across the room.

Freezing, I pulled away and turned to the television to see that one of the characters was shot, resulting in the sound that echoed loudly around my living room.

Turning back to Jack, immediately regret set in although some of it faded when I saw how dazed he look. "I-"

"No, don't regret it. I don't." He interrupted, his voice low and husky, effectively cutting me off and his hand reaching up to caress my lower lip with his thumb.

I eyed him warily, my heart was still racing and with an embarrassed moan, I quickly slid off his thighs when I realised I was still straddling him.

An amused smirk spread across his face and I took note with suppressed pride that his lips looked positively kissed. "But-" I started and got cut off - again - when Jack leaned towards me and covered my mouth with his hand.

"I like you Emma. I like you a lot. Actually for quite some time now but I can see that you have to think things through. But we will be talking about this alright?" He says seriously, his brown eyes staring at me with so much intensity that I was sure that I would have broken into goose bumps.

In all the months I've known Jack, I have never heard him speak with such seriousness in his voice. I could feel myself nodding my head as I fought the temptation to stare at the spot below his torso.

"Good. I'll drop by tomorrow if that is okay with you?"

Again, I could feel myself agreeing. I was probably too shocked by Jack's confession about his feelings towards me and the kiss that we just shared. Jack got to his feet and leaned down and pressed a gentle kiss on my forehead before exiting my house quietly leaving me still seated on the sofa stunned beyond belief.

What the hell have I gotten myself into?

* * *

A/N: Hey guys! An early update for you dears! I hope that you guys loved it and I was so motivated by your comments (from the previous chapter) to complete this one ASAP because this was something I think most of you guys couldn't wait.

Please vote and comment? I love you all and thanks for reading!

Chapter 16-The Reveal

Chapter 16-The Reveal

Jack Donnahue's POV

It was mind-blowing.

The kiss with Emma was everything I thought it would be and yet it was also better than I had thought. Of course, I had been fantasising about kissing her for days, well to be honest, weeks.

I had never thought that our little movie marathon would lead to that but I didn't regret it. But I now suspected - and feared - that Emma would be the one to regret our kiss. And I knew she would. But I was pleasantly surprised that Emma had kissed me back and who knew that she was such a good kisser?

Now, I was on my way to Emma's home and I was anxious as hell for her reaction. Was she going to tell me that we could only be friends? I couldn't, especially not after that kiss we shared yesterday.

Once I reached the house, I quickly threw on my cap and sunglasses on before exiting my car. Just as I was about to knock the door, the door opened and Emma stepped out, her eyes wide as she looked at me.

"What are you doing here?" She questioned hurriedly as she tugged Ella with her.

I stared at her warily, some hint of panic rising in my chest Was she going to chase me away? "You said we would talk about yesterday..." I trailed off and a smirk appeared on my face as Emma's face turned red. "Right... Would it be okay if you came by later? I have to go to the museum to grab some files and Ella's babysitter won't be around."

"I could watch Ella till you're back." I offered quickly and shoved my hands into my pockets as Ella waved cheerily at me and I offered her a wide grin.

"I don't know," Emma chewed on her lower lip, the bottom lip that I had bit lightly on just yesterday. Immediately, I could feel heat flushing onto my neck and I pushed that image out of my head. "Why not? We could watch a movie right Ella? Or we could play with your dolls."

Ella started cheering in agreement and Emma shot me a flat stare, immediately knowing that I had won. "Alright. I'll be back at most in thirty minutes."

I nodded and Emma sighed and stepped out of the doorway and unconsciously pressed a kiss on my cheek. "Thanks, I won't be long." With that she was gone.

I was thankful that she didn't turn around to see the silly grin on my face. It meant something right? If she kissed me on my cheek. It wasn't on my mouth, but hey, it was something.

"Alright Lala, what do you want to do?" I questioned playfully as Ella burst into giggles at my nickname for her. "Watch a movie! My dolls are taking a nap and they need rest."

"That's right. When they are tired, they need their naps," I said seriously before settling onto the sofa and Ella crawled onto the seat and sat beside me.

"What do you want to watch?" I questioned and Ella shrugged as I slowly flicked the channels. Suddenly, while I was changing the channels, Ella squealed excitedly, her long pigtails flying as she caught sight of the action film playing on the screen.

"That's daddy!"

I squinted my eyes to peer at the said figure that little Ella was pointing to on the screen of the television and my jaw dropped. "Huh? What do you mean Ella?" I questioned stupidly, wondering if I heard the five-year-old correctly. I had to be hearing things didn't I?

Ella shot me an unimpressed look that only kids could pull off before repeating. "That's my daddy but Aunt Emma says he's not well so I can't see him."

My heart felt like it was beating at an irregular speed and my stomach felt like someone had punched me in the gut. I couldn't even believe what I was hearing and I was wondering if I was in some alternate reality where things didn't make sense. A world where Ella was Theo Heywood's daughter.

Immediately, my mind was racing and I felt breathless. "Theo Heywood is your father?" I asked slowly, my mind was trying to wrap around this fact but loads of things still didn't make sense.

"Uh huh. Mummy didn't want me and gave me to Aunt Emma."

I blinked at that, unsure of how to reply to that and studied Ella carefully. It was sad that someone didn't want someone as amazing as Ella was and I briefly wondered who was her mother. But whoever she was, she was an idiot for giving Ella up.

Never mind, there were other things to think about. Emma had said that her brother was in a coma...Did that make her Theo Heywood's sister?!

I had met Theo Heywood before and I thought that he was pretty decent despite his famous status and it came as a shock that he was in a coma due to overdosing of drugs. He didn't seem like the type. From that only encounter, he seemed pretty grounded and I had no clue that he was into drugs.

But if Theo had a daughter, one that was amazing and brilliant like Ella, why did he turn to drugs? It didn't seem like his character but then again, I didn't know him well. But the whole situation was pretty sad and the only victim was Ella.

Another thought pushed the current one out of my mind and my jaw dropped at it. My mind had been too occupied about Ella and Theo but now, my brain was fixed on Emma.

Emma Greywood.

The girl that I really liked. If that was even her real name. My jaw clenched and I contemplated confronting Emma about it but I changed my mind. Knowing Emma, she wouldn't take that too well and I learned my lesson from the issue about Ella months ago.

Maybe everything was just a silly but startling coincidence. Maybe Emma was Theo's step-sister or she was adopted or something like that. But I knew I couldn't relax until this whole matter was cleared up.

Settling back onto the couch with Ella seated beside me, her attention fixed on the screen, I whipped out my phone and googled 'Emma Greywood'. I was half-hoping that everything I've just found was a coincidence and that the girl I was half-in love with hadn't been lying to me about her identity.

But because life was a bitch - especially to me, there wasn't a single thing about an Emma Greywood except a small profile about her job in the museum website that she was working in.

Clenching my jaw, I forced the irritation aside and reluctantly googled for Theo Heywood's wikipedia page. Immediately, the picture of a handsome smiling dark haired man appeared and I stopped before peering closely at Ella.

The resemblance was uncanny. There was no doubt that Ella was his daughter. The only thing that the five-year-old hadn't inherited from the actor was her pale blonde hair. Other than that, every little feature she had came from Theo Heywood.

Something heavy that felt like lead settled into the pit of my stomach when I noticed the sibling section on Theo Heywood's Wikipedia page.

Emmaline Grey Heywood.

That heavy feeling disappeared and it was replaced with the sensation of having all the breath in my body being knocked out with a baseball bat.

My thumb hovered over the link, hesitation was evident as I argued with myself. Did I really want to know? Would it be alright if I checked it myself? Should I wait and ask Emma about it?

In the end, the part of me that was determined to know won and before I could change my mind, I pressed the link.

The results came out and I inhaled sharply. There wasn't a doubt that Emmaline Grey Heywood and Emma Greywood were the same person. However, the images that appeared had little resemblance to the woman I knew.

The pictures showed a teenager with shocking blonde hair and the girl hardly resembled Emma. But somehow, there were slight similarities. The light hazel colour of her eyes was one and the same facial features were there but other than that, there weren't anything to say that they were the same woman.

Studying the pictures closely, I finally noticed the difference. The Emma I know had a more serious demeanour and didn't have the carefree and lighthearted one that her younger self had.

I scrolled further down and my brows raised in surprise to read that Emma was a former model and a child actress. However an image of an awful car accident appeared and my eyes widened at that sight, the car didn't even resemble a car, the metal was all scrunched up and there were shards of glass littering the road and there were numerous pools of blood on the road.

Emma had been in that accident?

Good god, it was a miracle she had survived. However scrolling through all the articles, there wasn't one that was recent. The latest one was dated about five years ago and it had been questioning the current whereabouts of her.

From the few pieces of information I had gleaned from the articles, it was safe to say that ever since that accident, Emma hadn't been seen in public. But why?

However, anger flared up at me at the thought of being lied to. Had Emma been deceiving me all along? Was I a way for her to get back into Hollywood?

No, Emma detested the publicity I had and she always tried to avoid going out with me in public in fear that she would be reported on. The very thought of her using me to get famous was ridiculous when she was running away from it.

However, now that I knew her real identity, everything made so much sense. The refusal to talk about her family, the absence of any personal and family objects in her house, the name change - though I thought it was a poorly changed one.

I was shocked about what I had discovered. Who wouldn't be? In fact, that very word wasn't enough to describe what I was feeling. It was practically an understatement. The anger faded but it was replaced with irritation and hurt and I felt a little like a fool.

Clenching my jaw, I shut my eyes and leaned my head back onto the couch, the sounds of the movie was still playing. My head was swirling with all the information and news I had gotten.

The irritation and hurt that I was feeling was due to Emma keeping secrets from me but I understood her reasons. Why would she divulge them to me? I was just someone she had met by accident and Emma had only known me for a few scant months.

Despite understanding her reasons, I was still a little upset and hurt about it. But the revelation from today didn't changed how I felt about her. I still liked her and kissing her yesterday made my feelings for her intensify.

Now the only thing I had were questions. Was Emma estranged from her family? How many people knew about Ella? Who was Ella's mother? Did Zach know about Emma's secret? Why did Emma leave Hollywood? Should I ask Emma about it? And should I let her know that I knew?

I drummed my fingers on my thigh, deep in thought before giving up. No, I would wait for her to tell me in her own time. A small slither of a doubt crept into my mind. Would she even tell me about her past? And what if she had no intention of doing so?

No, I was sure that Emma would tell me. Though I suspected that it would take her quite some time for her to do so.

I didn't have any more time to contemplate about the dilemma I was in as the door opened and Emma stepped in, her hands full of files. "Hey, has Ella been good?"

"Yes I have!" Ella hollered and ran after Emma who was currently in the kitchen. Switching the television off, I joined them slowly, still unsure of what to do.

But now, seeing Emma in the flesh after discovering her secret, it certainly didn't change the way I felt about her. Instead, I was even more impressed. Not about the hiding and all, that still stung. But how she managed to start anew and raise Ella.

I shoved my hands into my pockets and leaned against the doorframe as Ella began chattering away to Emma who entertained her questions while packing up the mess of crayons and drawing paper all over the table. Suddenly, an odd feeling hit me in the chest and looking at the scene in front of me, it felt rather...domestic.

Emma raised her head and caught me staring at her and a faint flush heated up her cheeks before she quickly ducked her head down. "Ella, I think your dolls are awake from their nap. I can hear them calling for you."

Immediately, Ella perked up and raced out of the kitchen and to her room, leaving Emma and I alone in the room. Now, all I wanted to do was stride up to her and kiss her again but I guessed she wouldn't encourage that seeing that we needed to talk.

"Jack," she paused and lifted her head to meet my gaze, "I don't know what to say. I-"

"Emma, I like you a lot and I have for these past few months despite you insisting on being just friends. And I know you like me too, if not you wouldn't have kissed me back yesterday. So, would you go out with me?" I asked quickly, trying to hide my anxiousness by crossing my arms over my chest.

For once, Emma seemed to be at a loss for words and all she did was gape at me for what seemed like hours when in reality, it was about mere seconds.

She chewed on her lower lip, and once again, I resisted the urge to pull her towards me and ravish her. "Jack, I don't regret kissing you but I don't think I can go out with you."

Panic began to rise and my chest felt tight. Feigning casualness, I strode towards Emma until she was just right in front of me. "Why not? You like me enough to kiss me."

Emma pursed her lips and tucked her hair behind her ear, her hazel eyes not meeting mine. "I have responsibilities like Ella." she replied quietly.

I forced myself not to roll my eyes, knowing that Emma was giving crap excuses now that I knew what she had been hiding. "Right...What do I have to do to convince you?" I questioned softly and cupped the side of her face before stroking my thumb on the apples of her cheek.

Emma's eyes widened as thy finally met mine. Hearing no response, I leaned down and pressed my lips against hers softly. Slowly, I began moving my lips against her and my hand left her cheek before pulling her towards me until we were chest to chest.

Wrapping my arms around her waist, I began kissing her thoroughly while her hands slowly tangled themselves in my hair and I couldn't help but let a smirk smugly appear on my face. Emma pushed me away and I couldn't help my gaze drift down to her lips that were a little red and swollen from our kiss.

"Jack, I-"

Once more, I interrupted her, "I know you're afraid of the news and publicity you might gain but we'll try to keep things quiet alright? Just take a risk, what have you got to lose?"

Emma stared at me, her eyes watching me carefully while her face was like a blank mask; I couldn't tell what she was thinking. Inwardly, my heart was beating so fast, in fear that she would still turn me down and tell me to get lost.

It felt like an eternity, the silence that is. I was just about to step away in defeat when she gave a short curt nod before saying quietly. "Okay. I'll go out with you."

Bloody fucking yes!

Elation swept across me like a tidal wave and a wide grin spread across my face, "Really?"

Emma nodded and was about to turn away but my hold on her waist tightened and I pressed her back against the table and kissed her. My tongue swept across her lower lip before deepening the kiss. Emma's hands wrapped themselves around my neck as she met my kiss with equal eagerness.

Once we stopped for breath, I leaned my forehead against hers before grinning roguishly, "So do I call you girlfriend now?"

Emma stared at me evenly but I could see her lips twitching from trying to suppress laughter and I quirked up an eyebrow which resulted in a short laugh from her. "I don't think so. You haven't taken me out for a date yet."

"Oh, I haven't, had I?" I grinned as a teasing smile appeared on Emma's face and she shrugged before pushing me away from her. "I don't recall anything happening," Suddenly, Emma's demeanour turned serious. "Jack, I really don't want anyone in the media knowing about me."

I nodded, I knew her reasons but I couldn't help but ask. "I know but why?"

"I'm a very private person," Emma explained as she reached for a grocery bag and continuing as she pulled out items from the paper bag. "I don't particularly like my life being dissected by strangers alright?"

"Yeah." I answered as I studied her face. For a moment, I had thought and hoped that she would come clean about everything to me but she didn't.

"Would you be staying for dinner?"

That brought me out of my slightly sombre mood and I grinned before leaning against the table. "Yes especially if you're going to cook wearing only an apron."

"Jack!"

I burst into raucous laughter and shot her a charming grin. "What? Am I not allowed to make jokes now?" All I received was an exasperated sigh and an eye roll.

Emma turned away from her bags of grocery that littered the table and moved her files away before pressing a kiss on my cheek. "Thanks for being understanding."

I nodded and smirked, "Of course. I'm your boyfriend, aren't I? That's included in the job description isn't it?"

Emma shrugged, "You're not my boyfriend until you've taken me out for more than one date." she gave me a teasing grin before stacking her files in a neat pile. "I really appreciate that you're being so understanding." she pressed a chaste kiss on my lips before starting to prepare dinner.

As I watched her, relief and ecstasy bloomed and I was just glad that she was mine.

Finally.

However, I just hoped that she would come clean about everything to me soon.

* * *

A/N: Here you go lovelies! I hoped this is able to satisfy your craving for more of the story to go along! It's way longer and about 3000+ words! Thanks so much for reading and please vote and comment! I love you all so much! And we are closer to 100k reads! Thanks so much for that! <3

Chapter 17-The Water Guns

Chapter 17-The Water Guns

Emmaline Heywood's POV

"Where exactly are we going?" I question a little nervously as Jack drove. It was about six in the evening and Jack had said that we would be heading out for a date in public.

I was a little nervous and paranoid that I would be recognised and the fact that Jack was still famous and we could get mobbed my screaming fans and reporters because I was sure that those disguises of Jack's wouldn't work all the time.

However, Jack had reassured me with a charming grin on his face before tugging me out of the house and opened the door for me. Ella's babysitter had come by to watch after her while we were out and to be very honest, I was a little intrigued with what Jack would come out for our first date.

Now, my main concern was Jack being recognised in public.

"Em, could you relax, I know you're still worrying about this, I can practically feel those worry waves all the way here." At that, I glared at him but Jack ignored me and continued cheerily," but like I said, I got it. I wouldn't be recognised." Jack announced confidently and I rolled my eyes.

"Fine. But at least tell me where we're going - Is that a fair?" I question as I caught sight of a ferris wheel.

"Yep! But its a masquerade themed fair. Patrons would have to wear a mask to enter. Apparently many celebrities come here and this fair specialises in keeping people's identities a secret."

I blinked and a reluctant smile tugged onto my face. "Really? Please don't tell me you got us masks already."

"How did you know?" Jack demanded, a frown wrinkling his face and I snorted, "It was a guess which I got right didn't I?"

Jack sighed heavily before parking the car. "Yes, it was meant to be a surprise and all but nooo, you had to guess. Whatever, here. This is yours." He handed me a pretty sky blue half-mask that had feathers and rhinestones on it. Carefully, I placed it over my face and when I turned to Jack, I almost choked from the mask he had on.

"Is that from the Phantom of the Opera?"

"Yep," he answered before placing a cap over his head before hopping out of the car. Shaking my head, I should have known Jack would get something theatric. I got out of the car and Jack tugged on my hand before pulling me over to the entrance. As we walked, I realised that his fingers were locked onto mine, his larger hand was almost enclosing my smaller one but I didn't protest.

Him holding onto my hand was...nice. Fighting back a blush, I quickened my pace and looked at Jack. He was right, with his cap on along with the mask, he was unrecognisable.

Paying for the tickets was easy, I handed the money to the man at the counter before Jack could bring his waller out and with that, we were in. "I wanted to pay," he grumbled and I spared him a glance. "You could pay for the food?"

"Alright. But this is a date, I'm your boyfriend, not a friend," Jack complained.

I quirked up an eyebrow (which I was sure Jack couldn't even see due to the mask I was wearing) and answered, "Yes but why not? What's wrong with me paying?"

Jack shot me a little smirk, "Because you're going to go home crying because I beat you in all of the carnival games."

"Oh really? Is that what you think?" I questioned indignantly and Jack shrugged, that irritating condescending smirk was still glued on his face. "Obviously, I'm the champion in my family." He blew out a breath and studied his nails before giving me a sly grin.

I narrowed my eyes and challenged, "Alright, we'll see. Let's go. NOW!" I ordered and tugged onto his arms and dragged him towards the nearest gaming booth.

"Oh Em, a water gun contest? Darling, I'm the king at that." Jack announced while rubbing his hands together in glee. The expression on his face was so comical that I wanted to burst out laughing but that would give the game away.

One thing Jack didn't know about me was that I was a really competitive person. This trait of mine was the very reason why Zach refused to play any sort of games with me or make any bets with me.

"Are we going to play or not?" I demanded and handed the store vendor some cash. Jack shrugged with a lopsided but yet smug grin on his face as he held onto the plastic water gun on my left. The purpose of the game was to hit as many metal targets as possible in the span of thirty seconds. The winner depending on the amount of targets hit would be able to choose a prize on the shelf.

Honestly, I could care less about the prizes on display seeing that they were all plush toys but I was winning for my pride and well, because I was competitive and wanted to see Jack's expression when I won.

"Game on darling," Jack said as he positioned himself but I ignored him and held onto the plastic gun, the familiarity of it almost made me grin but I restrained myself. When the buzzer rang which indicated that the game started, I began aiming and shooting at the metal targets.

It wasn't long till the buzzer rang and I placed the plastic gun back onto the counter and smirked triumphantly when I saw the results. I had managed to hit twenty-three targets while Jack managed twenty-one.

Beside me, Jack sputtered and turned towards me, his jaw had dropped to the ground and an awed expression took over. "B-but-I. How?!"

This time, I couldn't help but copy him and exhaled on my nails before examining them while feigning boredom. "It wasn't that difficult. In fact, it was like a breeze for me." Turning to the store vendor, I pointed to the stuffed toy that I wanted. It was a pink stuffed pig and I handed it to Jack with a smug grin on my face.

"Here's your consolation prize your majesty," I playfully mocked and Jack continued staring at me in shock.

Quickly, he snapped out of it and gave me a narrowed stare. "You know what? Thank you for this, but I want a rematch."

I raised an eyebrow as Jack placed the stuffed pig onto the counter beside me and I shrugged, "Alright." Typical male. Always insisting that they could not lose to women in silly games like this. I handed the vendor some cash again and the buzzer started.

Like before, I carefully aimed my gun at the metal targets before shooting and each time that it hit the target, a smirk formed on my face. It was about halfway throughout the game that I felt some water splashing on my face.

"What on earth?" I squealed and shook my head as I tried to squirm away from the source and when I looked up, Jack was aiming his water gun at me with a wicked and yet playful expression on his face.

"Jack! Why are you aiming at me? Hit the targets!" I demanded in annoyance but a playful smirk adorned his features as he continued shooting at me with the gun. By now, it was clear that Jack was ignoring me and was only focused on spraying me and hence, I did something that any sensible person would do if they were in my position.

I aimed the water gun back at him.

"Em! Come on! Give lil' old me a chance!" Jack crowed as he burst into laughter but I ignored him and continued my revenge by carefully aiming at his face before squeezing the trigger. Amusement bubbled up as I watched the jet of water hit his face and Jack sputtered while shielding his face from me. "Em! I'm out of water! Cut me some slack!"

Relentlessly, I continued aiming at him till the barrel of my gun was drained. When Jack finally realised why I had stopped, he grabbed hold of his water gun and I didn't realise what he was doing till it was too late. Jack had removed the barrel of his gun and it was half-filled with water and emptied it all over my head.

"JACK!"

At my shrieking, Jack burst into raucous laughter before lunging towards me and planted a sloppy kiss on my cheek. "You look like a little-drowned kitten, Em. It's cute."

I glared at him through my hair that was now all wet, "You wouldn't find me cute when I'm done with you!" I threatened and Jack planted another sloppy kiss on my cheek. "Nah, you like me way too much for that." With that, he wrapped an arm around my shoulders before passing twenty dollars to the store vendor who was looking quite annoyed with us messing about.

"Sorry about that, my girlfriend is just upset that I ate all her cheesecake when it was hers." Jack announced cheerily and the store vendor grumbled under his breath as he accepted the money. All I could hear was mumblings about 'stupid people' and 'idiots who wasted my time'.

With an arm around my shoulder, Jack led me away from the store before taking another glance at me and burst into noisy laughter. "Oh god, you really look like a drowned kitten with that angry expression on your face."

"Of course, since you got me all wet!" I growled while trying to wring the water out of my hair.

"Oh really? Did I?" Jack questioned, a wolfish but yet playful smirk on his face as he wriggled his eyebrows at me.

"What-Jack! Not that!" I hissed and tried to fight the smile appearing on my face. Somehow, Jack had this talent of his that always made me smile no matter the situation.

"Don't deny it. It's okay, that always happens whenever I'm around," he said offhandedly while leading me towards a hotdog stand that was quite far off and I rolled my eyes at that comment.

"But seriously, I'm drenched. My shirt is all wet," I grumbled, not liking the way my top clung to my body with that sensation of something slimy and cold on your body.

"I know. I can see your bra."

"What?"

Jack wriggled his eyebrows at me once more before smirking, "I'm kidding. You're wearing black for goodness sake. But I wouldn't mind-"

Snorting, I punched him playfully in the arm, "In your dreams Donnahue."

"I know. That's mine every night." I could feel myself flush and I was thankful that the sun had set and the only lights available were from the colourful decorations and street lamps so that he couldn't see me blushing.

Not knowing how to respond to that, I chose to ignore that and we continued strolling towards the hotdog stand. "You know what I really want to know? How are you so good at that game?" Jack questioned and I chewed on my lower lip.

"My brother used to go to this sort of fairs with me when I was younger," I replied quietly, the lightheartedness I had been experiencing dimmed a little at the thought of Theo.

I guessed Jack had sensed the change in the atmosphere as he quickly changed the subject. "Anyway, since we are here, have you spotted any celebrities you might know?"

My head turned towards him and I raised an eyebrow. "Really? You've seen some familiar faces despite the masks?"

"Yeah, one or two but don't worry, they won't recognise me, I'm wearing a baseball cap."

I fought back the urge to snort a little at that. As if wearing a baseball cap would manage to hide your identity. "Right, anyway, after getting some hotdogs, what do you want to do? Rollercoasters?"

Jack seemed to brighten at that and as we sat down on the benches near the hotdog stand and I couldn't help but realise this was the most fun I had in quite some time.

* * *

"I hope you had fun," Jack offered and I could see that he was a little nervous as he waited for my response. I gave him a sincere smile. "I did, it was fun despite you splashing water on me."

Jack chuckled and gave me another lopsided smile, "You secretly don't mind, do you?"

I rolled my eyes but I could feel a hint of a smile playing on my lips, "If that's what makes you sleep better."

Now, it was about eleven and we were outside my house. By now, I was sure that Ella was asleep and her babysitter was waiting till I got home. A sense of anticipation crawled onto me when Jack stared at me, his dark eyes darted to my lips and I swear that my heart skipped a beat.

"Thank you for bringing me out today, I had a lovely time," I blurted out and Jack let out a low laugh and one of his hands reached out to touch my face. His hand cradled my cheek while his thumb caressed the top of it and I couldn't help but feel a shiver go down my spine at his touch.

"I'm glad you had fun," he answered quietly, his lips inching closer to mine and I parted my lips and he was so close-

The door opened and I jumped before whirling around to see Bethany, Ella's babysitter staring at us with an amused and yet questioning look.

"Sorry to interrupt, I saw you outside and I uh-"

I shook my head and offered a tight smile. "Yeah its fine. You can go now." Bethany smiled before leaving and I looked up at Jack. Clearly, the mood was gone and a sense of awkwardness had descended on us. Suddenly realising why Ella's babysitter had given us odd glances, it was due to the fact that both Jack and I have not removed our masks.

"I better get in before uh it's too late. Tomorrow is work day and all," I said softly, my cheeks heating up when I realised Jack was still staring at me with that intense stare in his dark eyes.

"Yeah of course. Have a goodnight," he called out as he shoved his hands into his pockets.

I nodded, "You have a goodnight too," and I shut the door before leaning my back against it. My heart was racing and I knew my cheeks were flushed.

Before I could leave, the sound of the door being knocked made me stop. Had Jack forgotten something? Or had I left something behind in his car?

Opening the door, I questioned, "Did you forget somethin-" but was met with Jack tugging me closer with his lips slanting over mine as he kissed me deeply.

My hands curled into his hair as if he was a lifeline in a storm and I kissed him back with equal fervour. Soon enough, Jack pulled away and flashed me a smirk before winking at me, "Yeah, I forgot that. Night Em."

Dazed from the kiss he had given me, I shook my head and went back into my house, trying my best not to smile and to forget that my lips were still tingling.

* * *

A/N: Hi guys, my exams are over and I'll be back to updating this quite often now! Maybe an update every 4-5 days! Thanks so much for sticking with me through this book despite the irregular updates and what not! Love you all and I hoped that you guys liked this chapter! <3

Chapter 18-The Discussions

Chapter 18-The Discussions

Jack Donnahue's POV

I frowned at the offending swatch colour that Daniella was holding below my face before complaining again, "I don't see why I have to follow your dress code for ties! Why can't I wear what I want?"

Gwennie who was sitting on the couch while I was standing in front of her as Daniella placed another swatch below my neck sniffed disdainfully, "Because Jack, I know you well. You're bound to mess something up, be it dress code or behavioural wise. And since I can't control your behaviour, I'll take charge of your suit on that day!"

I sulked and Gwennie screeched, "No! Not red! Jack doesn't look good in red!"

"Excuse me?" I started, offended before crossing my arms, "I look good in any colour. Right Emma?" I directed my last statement to my girlfriend to see that she wasn't paying me any attention.

"Sorry what?" she questioned as she looked up from her phone. "I look good in any colour right?" I stressed and gave her a beseeching look, practically begging her to agree with me. "Well," she paused before she glanced at my sister who was staring at her defiantly as if she was daring my girlfriend to disagree with her.

"Actually, I don't know. I'm not someone in the fashion industry like Gwendolyn who knows all this stuff. Jack you should listen to your sister, its her wedding after all." Emma explained smoothly and again, I admired her skill in placating both Gwennie and I at the same time.

Gwennie beamed and shot me a smug smirk, "Thank you Emma! There you go Jack. Now shut up so I can find an appropriate colour for you."

All I could do was roll my eyes and remain silent while glaring sullenly at the ground as Gwennie continued deciding with Daniella what colour suited me best.

As I stood there, bored out of my mind, my gaze wandered over to Emma who was watching Ella play with my niece nephews. Currently, we were at my house seeing helping Gwennie in preparing for her wedding with Zach. It was a little ridiculous that Zach wasn't around see that he was in another state for some historical convention or something like that. Hence, it was everyone in my family plus Emma who was here.

Right now, Isadora was calling the florist while Strider hovered nearby due to her reaching full-term, Daniella was helping Gwennie decide the colour ties for all of her brothers, Cameron was off calling the caterers and the hotel venues and Emmett was watching over the children.

"Alright, Jack you can go with Emma to help with the invitations," Gwennie ordered as she gestured towards the stack of pristine white envelopes with blue ribbons on the table.

"You're kidding right," I said flatly and Gwennie glared back at me in response and I grumbled under my breath before heading towards the table with Emma already there.

"You should lighten up, it's your sister's wedding to my best friend, I might add."

I sighed and watched Emma take a ribbon before tying it on the flap of the envelope before deciding to do the same lest Gwennie started screaming at me. "Yeah, I know. But just think of what we could be doing now if we didn't have all this stuff to do."

Emma snorted a little before her eyes met mine with amusement, "Sure, I'll be at the museum working. And speaking of work, why don't you have any movies to act in or something like that?"

I shrugged and furrowed my brows as I tried to replicate the perfect bow that Emma had done on the envelope before giving up. "I have one upcoming, filming starts in September."

"You slacker," Emma teased and I smirked in response, "Gives me more time to bring you out for dates."

Again, Emma snorted as she started shaking her head, "No thanks, if I'm going to get soaked again."

At that, I couldn't help but burst into laughter at that suggestive statement and by the pinkness in her cheeks, I could safely say that Emma had realised what that sounded like.

"Aunt Emma! Look!" Ella squealed excitedly as she ran towards us with a piece of paper which looked like drawings on it. "This is for you! Hi Jack!" she greeted toothily before giving the paper to Emma.

"Hello Lala, don't I have one too?" I questioned while feigning hurt with a hand clasped onto my chest dramatically. Ella gasped and a expression which was a mix of shock and horror crossed her face before she hurried off to draw one for me as well and I burst into laughter. "God, she's hilarious."

Emma smiled before sliding the drawing carefully into her bag before commenting lightly, "You're really good with her." I shrugged and slid the envelope to the right before replying, "Well, I have a niece and almost three nephews, you've got to be good with kids."

"Right," Emma said and focused on tying the ribbons, "you're just really good with them. It's a gift."

"You're good with Ella too," I pointed out. Emma gave me a wry smile, "Only because she's my niece, I'm not really good with children to be honest."

"Well, I for one think that you don't give yourself enough credit. You raised Ella on your own and I think you've done a fantastic and incredible job."

Emma smiled at my words before she turned back to her envelopes and responded quietly, "Thank you."

* * *

"What's wrong?"

Isadora frowned as she pursed her lips while drumming her fingers on the table. "Nothing. Don't worry about it," she said as she studied her brother-in-law Jack who was grinning at his quasi-girlfriend Emma.

"Don't give me that," Strider said sternly while flipping through a stack of files that he had brought along. Isadora shrugged before laying her head back on the wall, "It's nothing. It's just that Jack's girlfriend Emma reminds me of someone."

Without hesitating, Strider replied nonchalantly as he scanned the lengthy document in his hands as he gave his wife a distracted answer, "That's what you say about everyone. Also, that's the same thing you said about about my secretary."

"So? Just look at her! Can you honestly tell me she doesn't look familiar to you?" Isadora demanded and crossed her arms with difficulty due to her very pregnant belly. Hearing the no-nonsense tone that he knew not to argue with (unless it was something serious), Strider met her gaze evenly before giving his brother's girlfriend a quick glance.

"No, she's pretty enough and certainly too smart for Jack but I've never seen her before in my life," he answered honestly before turning his attention back to his files.

"Men, you lot are hopeless. I swear that I have seen her somewhere before. This is making me really annoyed until I want to hit my head on the wall till I get it!" Isadora grumbled and continued drumming her fingers on the table, her eyes still on Emma who was fighting back a laugh at Jack's antics.

"Don't do that. You're pregnant," Strider automatically said and Isadora raised her eyebrows in a challenge before retorting with a smirk on her face. "Well you fucked me into the wall the last time and I'm fine."

Without missing a beat, Strider responded patiently as he flipped a page, "That was before I knew you were pregnant, hence, it doesn't count."

Isadora snorted and shifted in her seat. Her back was aching, her feet was aching, hell her head was aching but she couldn't help but bait her husband. "Well, what exactly was last night?" she purred, her tone now low and husky.

Again, her husband responded smoothly, "That was me giving you a foot massage which turned into something more until we got interrupted by our son." "Well that's true." Isadora sighed in resignation before resting her chin on her palm as she studied Jack who was now giving lopsided and charming grins while Emma replied with a small smile on her face. "Jack seems very happy."

"He's always happy."

"No, not his usual happy, he seems happy. Like really really happy." Isadora said and her tone made Strider stop reading his cases before he turned to his wife but the expression on her face made him turn his attention to his second youngest brother.

"I see," Strider commented and seeing the lovestruck expression on Jack's face made a rare smile appear on his face. "He looks like how I did when I proposed to you."

Isadora snorted a laugh before shooting her husband a bemused stare, "Which one? The first attempt or the second one?"

Strider narrowed his eyes at her and he knew he could feel himself flush. It was a never-ending joke in the Donnahue household that Strider had made a fool of himself when he had blurted out a request for Isadora to marry him when they were merely friends with benefits. Or more like acquaintances with benefits.

Strider knew that his wife would hold it over his head for the upcoming years and yet, he didn't particularly mind. At least he didn't made a mess of his proposal like Cameron did.

"Both."

Isadora softened and smiled before leaning towards him to press a kiss on his cheek. "You old softy," she grinned and got to her feet, "I'm going to the bathroom, don't worry about me."

Strider rolled his eyes and he turned back to his files but not giving his brother Jack one last glance. Yes, the besotted expression on his face was all Strider needed to know. He only hoped that everything worked out well for him.

Flipping to another page, Strider frowned before making a mental note to correct some errors before hands slammed down on the table in front of him, causing some of the papers to fall to the floor.

"Isa-"

"I think I know who she is already!"

* * *

"You know, you're probably the only woman who didn't even want to be friends with me," I started and Emma scoffed before tying a perfect ribbon on the envelopes. "You really are, that's why I was so interested in you until I realised you're my dream girl."

Emma raised her eyebrows sceptically as she slid the pristine white envelope to the left before taking another one in her hands, "Really? How exactly would you describe someone like that?"

I could feel myself flushing as I tied a not so perfect ribbon on the envelope. "That's for me to know," I said evenly before changing the subject, "Anyway, how long more do we have to do this? My fingers hurt!" I grumbled half-heartedly and Emma rolled her eyes and passed me more envelopes and ribbons in response.

"Your sister Gwendolyn insisted that we finish this by today."

I gaped at the tall mountain of envelopes and the pile of ribbons before groaning out loud. Emma ignored me but I could feel her eyes glancing towards me occasionally.

That only happened when she wanted to ask me something and I knew better to question her directly. And soon enough, Emma called out, "Jack?"

"Hmm?"

"Why do you consider me your dream girl?"

Was it me or was there a hint of guilt in her tone? Was she feeling terrible that she had not told me the truth about her real identity? Or was I just simply imagining it?

Also, I didn't particularly want to answer that, it was way too embarrassing and I was pretty sure Emma would freak out. Thankfully, Isadora stopped by our table and sat down in between us and let out a sigh of relief. "God, I can't wait till the baby is out, he's actually killing me."

I snorted, "Maybe he knows his favourite uncle is nearby."

Isadora scowled at me before tossing her hair behind her shoulders, "Right, anyway, how are the both of you doing? If Gwennie tells me to help decide on seating plans again, I'm going to kill her."

Emma cracked a smile at that before continuing to tie the red ribbons onto the envelopes containing the invitations. "I'll pay to see that," I mumbled under my breath and Isadora let out a cackle as she heard me.

"Enough about that, so Emma, how is it like dating Jack? Trying? Irritating?"

"Isadora, if you don't shut up, Strider will find himself a widower!" I hissed and glared but this time, Isadora wasn't even looking at me, her gaze was fixed on Emma and a bad feeling filled the pit of my stomach.

Emma paused and she looked up at Isadora with an arrogant tilt to her head, "Quite the opposite actually."

I eyed the two women sitting on the same table warily and wondered if I should call Zach over for some help because I had no idea what was going on and what to do.

"Well, that's good. At least you can be another pair of eyes to watch Jack if he becomes an alcoholic or a...drug user."

My heart felt like it stopped and I couldn't believe what I was hearing. Does Isadora know about Emma's actual identity and what the hell did she think she was doing? Glancing at Emma, my heart raced uncomfortably when I spotted that her entire body froze and her face went blank.

"Isadora, enough!" I gritted my teeth, she was ruining everything!

"I trust that Jack isn't that foolish to do those activities," Emma replied flatly and her brown eyes flashed defiantly at Isadora but I could see that her eyes had a glint of suspicion in them.

Fuck fuck fuck.

"Well that is true, Jack isn't that stupid or he knows we're all going to come after him, right Emma? Or should I call you Emmaline?"

Bloody fucking hell.

"Isadora shut up!" I growled and my eyes snapped to Emma who was frozen like a statue. Her eyes flickered between Isadora and I before she pressed her lips into a thin line while her face gave away nothing. It was like a blank canvas and I couldn't tell what was going on in her mind but all I knew was, this was not going to turn out in my favour.

"You don't seem surprised Jack, I'm guessing you already knew," she said and her eyes hardened a little. Fucking hell. "Em wait," I started and stood up to reach out for her when she grabbed her bag and called for Ella before disappearing.

All I could feel was the sinking feeling in my stomach as I stared at the direction she had gone.

* * *

A/N: Hello lovelies! Here's another update and I hope you guys love it, please comment and vote! Thank you so much for reading and I love you all! <3

Chapter 19-The Heart-To-Heart

- -

Chapter 19-The Heart-To-Heart

Emmaline Heywood's POV

I should have known.

I should have bloody well known it.

Should've known that nothing in my life would be smooth sailing. Why didn't I see it earlier? And how long had Jack known about everything? And since when did he know?

It did explain a lot on how he seem to be waiting for something every time he was around me. It wasn't obvious, it was subtle and I had initially dismissed it as him being unsure about my reaction to him. But I was wrong. I was so stupid. How the hell could I have not seen it? Currently, I was so tempted to hit my head against the wall or something equally hard for not seeing it sooner but it was too late.

Now, the questions I had was; how much did he know? And what would happen to Ella and I? A brief moment of panic had made me wonder if Jack would go to the press but I had dismissed it. If that was his intention, he would have done it the moment he found out and besides, he wasn't the type to get attention. He was already famous enough just for being seen in a cafe.

Also, another part of me wondered if Jack had not known, would I even tell him about it? And that part made me feel guilty. Because deep down, I knew I wouldn't. So basically, our relationship would be based on lies on my part.

I was conflicted as hell.

And the anxious feeling in my gut hadn't abated ever since Ella and I left after Isadora brought the whole issue up. Another question was; how did Isadora know? Had Jack confided in her? And now, where did Jack and I stand?

I sighed heavily and flipped through the folders from work to try to distract myself from everything that had occurred in the last twenty-four hours. It was about four hours since I left and up till now, Jack hadn't even contacted me. Did that mean that we were no longer together?

I could feel my heart sinking deeper as each minute passed and I knew everything was going to change. Grabbing another folder, I shifted on the chair before forcing myself to focus on my work, it was utterly useless in trying to anticipate something or worry about it there I had no control of.

Just as I was able to read through the documents - without worrying - the doorbell rang. Furrowing my brows, I got to my feet and glanced at the clock in the dining room. It was almost eleven and I couldn't imagine who would be at the door.

Could it be Jack? My heart rate sped up at that and when I opened the door, it really was him.

"Hey, may I come in?" he greeted hopefully while running his fingers through his hair.

Without thinking, I blurted out, "Why?"

Why was I such an idiot every time I was around him? Before I could take that back, Jack's happy demeanour seem to sink a little as he replied hesitantly, "We need to talk."

Not trusting myself to say anything sensible, I chewed on my lower lip before nodding and swung the door wider so that he could come in.

He entered the living room and stopped at the photo frames I had put back in their original place. No point in hiding them when he already knew right? "You're cute as a kid," he commented lightly with his hands shoved into the pockets of his jeans.

A small reluctant smile crossed my face at that, "Everyone is cute as a kid," I replied a little awkwardly as I wrung my hands together. Deciding to get this talk over and done with, I settled on the couch and asked, "How long have you known?"

Jack stared down at me before he ran his fingers through his hair making it even more tousled than before when he replied quietly, "That day when I babysat Ella while you went back to the museum to get your work. Ella and I were watching an action a movie and she pointed out the actor that was her father and I connected the dots."

"Oh," I murmured with my gaze on the ground, "That was about three weeks ago. Why didn't you confront me about it?"

Jack exhaled heavily, "Because I figured that this was something you should tell me in your own time, it wasn't any of my business to ask and I was waiting for you to tell me not that it matters now anyway."

I remained silent and I felt a little touched that he thought that way but also, the guilt intensified. "I see, so how much do you know about me?"

Jack studied me, his brown eyes roving over my face as if he was checking to see if I was testing him or anything - which I wasn't - before he answered honestly, "About your real name and that you were a former model and actress, your twin brother Theo, the accident and well that's it."

I nodded and lifted my feet onto the sofa and hugged them tightly with my arms before saying softly, "I'm sorry that I didn't tell you everything earlier and that you had to find out this way."

"Why didn't you tell me?"

Was that hurt in his voice? Guilt swarmed up even more and I pressed my lips into a thin line. "I didn't really see the point. My real name may be Emmaline Heywood but she died in that car crash. I'm Emma Greywood now. Besides, why would I even want to talk about the foolish self I had been?"

His eyes were fixed on me, waiting for me to continue and I let out a bitter laugh, "The only thing I gained from my life in Hollywood was useless cash and scars."

"Scars from the accident?" he asked cautiously and I nodded. Watching Jack's face, I could see a range of emotions over his face from shock to sympathy and then to a little of pity. Quickly, I forced myself to look away and focus on the fabric of my tights instead. I refused and absolutely abhorred being pitied on. Both sympathy and empathy was fine but pity? No. Never.

"I don't want your pity Jack, I assume you saw the pictures of the crash?" I questioned bitterly and beside me, I could sense that he was a little hesitant in replying but he did so anyway, "Yes, I'm just horrified that you were in that thing and it's a miracle that you're okay."

"I wasn't. Not at first. I almost lost the ability to walk and did you know what was the first thing my mother said to me when I was awake from the surgery? She said 'It's a pity that she has scars, that modelling career is gone now.' And the next thing she said was to tell me to get plastic surgery."

Jack remained quiet and his eyes watched me with an intensity that could set anything aflame. "I went into depression for a year and Theo, my brother - my only family member - supported me along with Zach. My parents did nothing but soak up the attention that I had gained from my accident. And that was when I knew, I had to leave Hollywood."

By now, I could feel the sting in my eyes that was the telltale sign of tears and god, I hated crying, especially in front of someone. And especially in front of Jack.

Fighting the tears back, I inhaled sharply and set my shoulders back, I was not weak, I would not cry. I guess Jack could sense that I was near to tears because he tugged me gently into his arms and the warmth of him comforted me. "You don't have to tell me-"

Shaking my head, I interrupted, "No, I should. I owe you an explanation. After all, you should have known before we got together."

"Alright, only if you want to tell me," he said quietly as he rubbed soothing patterns on my thigh as I leant onto him. "After I realised that I wanted out, my parents disowned me," I started and Jack tightened his arms around me at that. Continuing, "It's safe to say, I don't have parents now and Theo along with Zach had supported me with every decision I had made.

Anyway, I had gotten a scholarship in university and here I am today," I finished with a sniffle.

Silence reigned in the room and I guessed the reason why Jack was so quiet was because he was slowly digesting whatever I had told him. "I'm sorry that all this had happened to you," he offered softly and cradled me gently into his arms.

"It's okay. I'm used to it," I replied wistfully and Jack shifted me so that I was facing him with his arms still around me. "Well, now you have me too."

I stared at him shocked. I honestly wasn't expecting that. My heart was racing and my stomach felt like it was full of butterflies and I couldn't believe he had said that. Did it mean that he wanted to stick around.

But then again, reality crashed around me and I knew he couldn't. Because someone amazing like Jack didn't deserved to be stuck with me. I was cynical, stubborn, a pessimist and Jack deserved someone better. Obviously, I wasn't going to be that person.

"Thank you for listening to me," I offered quietly, not wanting - or knowing how - to respond to that statement of his.

Jack grinned down at me, "Of course, I'm your boyfriend aren't I? That's what we do for our girlfriends."

A reluctant smile crossed my face at that but I quickly looked away while tucking a stray curl behind my ear as I tried to ignore the warmth feeling that sentence brought me. Quickly forcing the smile back, I lifted my head so that our eyes could meet before saying, "I think we shouldn't be together."

Immediately, Jack froze and he frowned, "What? Why not?"

I blinked back hot tears, the subject that I was going to bring up always brought me to tears no matter how long ago it happened despite me accepting it. "Because you don't deserve to be stuck with someone like me-"

"Someone like you? Do you mean brilliant? Funny? Absolutely breathtaking?" he interrupted and if it was possible, his hold on me was tighter and all I could do was press my lips into a thin line to try to hold the tears back while trying not to believe the lovely things Jack thought of me.

"I can't give you what you want Jack!" I burst out and Jack furrowed his brows as he tried to figure out what I meant. "What are you talking about? To me you're perfect."

That was the last thing I knew before the tears started rolling down my cheeks. He thought I was perfect? I was definitely anything but that.

"I can't give you children Jack," I said quietly and again, more tears welled up in my eyes.

"What?" he stopped and stared at me but I couldn't look back at him. I didn't want to see the disappointment in his eyes or how he'll slowly shutter himself away from me.

"The accident also took away the ability for me to have children," I repeated and fidgeted before playing with the hem of my shirt. "I know you well Jack, at some point in your life, you'll want to have children on your own. I've seen you with your niece and nephews and not to mention Ella. And I can't give them to you and later, you'll start to resent me for it and I can't dea-"

I was cut off when his right hand clasped over my mouth, preventing me from speaking and due to the sudden action and all I could do was stare up at him with wide eyes.

"Listen, it doesn't matter to me," Jack paused when he saw my expression before rolling his eyes and gave me a stern glare, "don't assume how I would feel in the future. I have enough niece and nephews with more coming from Gwennie and Emmett and there are other options like adoptions. All I know is that I want you. Children or not."

I was stunned. By now, the tears were like a waterfall and I was pretty sure snot was everywhere as well and I was also certain I looked ridiculous. "But-" I began but got cut off - again.

"No buts, I mean it. I want you Emma or Emmaline. But I'll think I'll stick with Em - it's shorter." At that, I let out a snort which sounded a little off due to my tears and not to mention the snot and Jack's arms were still around me as he hugged me tightly against him as if I was going to disappear if he didn't have any contact with me.

He continued, "I really do. I told you earlier, you're my dream girl." I raised an eyebrow, "Why do you call me that?"

He flashed me a charming grin before he started to list off, "You're brilliant, funny, gorgeous and you have that dry sense of humour and not to mention you keep me grounded. You balance me out, when I'm all goofy and full of nonsense, you're serious and practical," he finished and I could only stare at him, stunned.

I couldn't believe it. Without thinking, I threw my arms around his neck and hugged him tightly. Jack hugged me in return and I could feel him press a kiss on the top of my head.

After a while, he added in a light conversational tone, "And now I don't have to wear condoms." I rolled my eyes and smacked his chest half-heartedly as I recognised his attempt to make the sombre mood lighter.

"Don't be an idiot," I muttered and he chuckled lowly in response and we sat there in my living room in silence. By now, I had calmed down considerably and suddenly Jack spoke up, curiosity hinting in his voice, "If it's okay to ask...what caused the accident?"

I stiffened a little and Jack hastily said, "It's okay if you don't want to say..." he trailed off hesitantly and I shook my head.

"I was at a party and I caught my then boyfriend cheating and I told him that I was going to break up with him. He didn't like that and it didn't help he had been drinking heavily. He dragged me to his car and started driving and he got angrier and angrier when I refused to cooperate and that is how the accident happened."

"What a dick," he gritted through his teeth and I shrugged, "It's in the past and I don't really want to talk much about it." Jack nodded and watched me carefully as he asked me, "We're still okay right?"

"Yes, if you'll have me," I replied softly and was rewarded with a brilliant smile from him.

"Good and yes, I'll still have you." With that, his lips met mine and I kissed him back slowly. The kiss was gentle and filled with tenderness and slowly, he pulled away and I rested my head on his shoulder.

Already, I could feel myself dozing off from the emotional turmoil I had gone through during the past few hours. Distinctly, I could hear him say that he should go but I had mumbled, "Stay."

"Alright," he replied and pressed another kiss on my forehead. Contented, I drifted off to sleep.

* * *

A/N: Hello, hope you all enjoyed this chapter and that you all liked it so please vote and comment? I'm not really too happy with this chapter, sigh. But I hope you lovelies liked it so please let me know what you think?

Chapter 20-The Argument

Chapter 20-The Argument

Jack Donnahue's POV

All I could feel was the sinking feeling in my stomach as I stared at the direction she had gone.

What the fuck just happened? Had I just lost Emma? Panic rose in my chest and I felt like I was going to be sick. I had the brief sensation of bile rising up my throat. How could everything crumble around me that quickly? Hadn't I taken precautions when I told her that I knew what she was hiding? Heck I even planned what to say! I had a script and everything!

Now?

My sister-in-law had ruined everything. Now Emma could probably be thinking that I was using her or something equally horrible as that. Clenching my fist, the only thought running through my head was that

Strider would officially be a widower. As of now. And that I had to fix somehow.

I had to.

"What the fuck was that?" I demanded harshly as I got to my feet and faced Isadora. I resisted the urge to wring her neck. But the fact that she was pregnant was a dead no.

"She was using you Jack! Don't be an idiot and be led around by your cock! She was just using you to get famous again after all these years! Tell me honestly you haven't thought about that at least once!"

I could feel myself flushing slightly because Isadora was right. Back when I first found out about Emma, the thought of her trying to use me for my fame did enter my mind. And I was ashamed because I knew Emma wasn't the sort to do that to people.

"You did didn't you? I can see it all over your face," she pointed out smugly with a hint of distaste in her tone.

Right now, I was very aware that everyone was watching and listening to get a clue on whats happening. And I was also very aware that my brother, Strider was approaching with a wary expression on his stern face. It was definitely due to the fact that I was on the verge of screaming at his - very - pregnant wife.

"That's not the point. It wasn't your place to say that and it wasn't any of your business! I knew all about it and I was waiting for her to tell me in her own time because it was her secret - not yours, so why the fuck did you think you had any right?" I sneered and glared down at her.

Isadora scoffed and crossed her arms over her chest, "What makes you so fucking sure she would tell you? To her, you may just seem like a tool. A tool for her to get back into Hollywood society!"

I snorted, "You don't know her like I do! Emma isn't the kind of person who would do that!"

Isadora got to her feet and tilted her chin defiantly, "How well do you even know her? About three to four months! That's not even enough time to say that you know someone well!"

"If my girlfriend is really an attention whore like you claim she is, she would have told the press months ago! That shows what you know; absolutely fucking nothing! Also, none of this isn't any of your business in the first place. And yes, I knew about it since approximately three weeks ago," I shot back and I could feel my hands clenching into fists.

Was this how rage felt like? I hadn't felt this upset before in my life. Sure I had gotten angry and yes, I had been furious. But I've never felt this much anger coursing through my veins before. In my opinion, I wouldn't even classify this as anger, it was much much more than that.

Isadora remained silent, her shoulders heaving and I could see that her eyes were blazing in anger. "You're too trusting Jack, it's like you never grew up! You're like a child!"

Something ugly welled up within me and I could feel my nails cutting into my palms from how hard I was clenching my hands; I was pretty sure the marks left behind would be there for quite sometime. And already, I knew I was going to say something unbearably harsh. It was one thing to claim that she was looking out for me, that I understood, even though it was none of her business. However, it was another thing to call me out and criticise me on my choices. I was an adult. I would be thirty this year and I could make my own damn decisions.

Who the hell did she think I was?

"Well, at least I'm not an insensitive bitch who didn't know when to shut the fuck up. Maybe you are the one who didn't grow up. Not everyone is like those horrid people you met in foster homes. Clearly you didn't leave that attitude you gained from growing up in one of those places," I spat and watched in horrid satisfaction as all the colour drained from Isadora's face at my words.

I could literally hear her inhale sharply and I knew I had hit a sore point but I didn't care. Although I felt a slight sting of guilt, the rage I felt at Isadora outweighed that. My sister-in-law had to understand and mostly accept that she couldn't be poking her nose in other people's business. Like mine.

Around me, I could see my siblings and their spouses raise their eyebrows or their dropped jaws. Their reaction could be due to me hardly showing anger or rage but I ignored them and quickly grabbed my cap and sunglasses along with my car keys before storming out of my own house.

Yes, my own damn house.

It was ridiculous, it should be the other way shouldn't it? Enough about that, I had to focus on damage control. I contemplated on immediately going to Emma's home but I knew I was too upset to do so. I was afraid that I would blurt something out and it would make everything worse.

No, it was best for the both of us and the situation that I wait before checking up on Emma. The very thought of losing both her and Ella made me feel nauseous and it felt like my heart would plummet to the very bottom of my gut. It certainly didn't help that my knees felt weak too.

And yes, I had grown to adore Ella. She was amazing and I was charmed by her. I knew that Emma had done a fantastic job of raising her properly.

Yes, I could not lose Emma.

I couldn't.

* * *

When I finally felt my anger simmer down, I took deep breaths before approaching Emma's home. I knew it was late but I didn't dare take the risks of talking to her tomorrow instead.

Knocking on the door, I rocked on my heels anxiously to wait for Emma to answer the door. Soon enough, she opened the door and she seemed vaguely surprised to see me.

"Hey, may I come in?" I greeted hopefully while running my fingers through my hair nervously.

"Why?"

God, she couldn't be turning me away could she? I could feel the faux happy expression on my face fade as I shoved my hands into the back pockets of my jeans. "We need to talk."

Fuck that sounded bad. We were already in a precarious situation and that sentence would make it worse. Fuck!

To my utter surprise, Emma gestured for me to enter and I could feel myself relax a little. As I entered the house, what made me stop was the sight of photo frames that hung on the walls and adorned places on the tables in her living room.

I knew the pictures weren't there before but the very sight of them made me stop and stare. The pictures portrayed Emma in her childhood with a boy whom I guessed was Theo Heywood. "You're cute as a kid," I commented just to fill up the awkward space in the room.

A small reluctant smile crossed her face at that, "Everyone is cute as a kid," she answered as she settled on the couch, "How long have you known?"

I stared down at her and swallowed harshly, "That day when I babysat Ella while you went back to the museum to get your work. Ella and I were watching an action a movie and she pointed out the actor that was her father and I connected the dots."

"Oh," she mumbled, "That was about three weeks ago. Why didn't you confront me about it?"

Settling on the couch beside her, I exhaled heavily before answering her, "Because I figured that this was something you should tell me in your own time, it wasn't any of my business to ask and I was waiting for you to tell me not that it matters now anyway."

My eyes remained fixed on Emma and I could see that she was visibly nervous and a little out of sorts and she was silent for a while before she finally replied. "I'm sorry that I didn't tell you everything earlier and that you had to find out this way."

"Why didn't you tell me?" God, I sounded so needy.

An expression that seemed like guilt appeared on her face and suddenly, a shutter seemed to block all her emotions away. "I didn't really see the point. My real name may be Emmaline Heywood but she died in that car crash. I'm Emma Greywood now. Besides, why would I even want to talk about the foolish self I had been?"

Emma let out a bitter laugh before continuing and I've never heard her sound so cynical since meeting her and it threw me off balance a little. "The only thing I gained from my life in Hollywood was useless cash and scars."

"Scars from the accident?" I asked hesitantly and Emma nodded in response.

I didn't know how to respond to that. I couldn't apologise, it would seem like pity and I knew Emma well enough that she had pride. Buckets full of it in fact and she wouldn't like it. And I guessed I was more transparent than I thought because Emma called me out on it.

"I don't want your pity, Jack, I assume you saw the pictures of the crash?"

"Yes, I'm just horrified that you were in that thing and it's a miracle that you're okay." I breathed out and it was true. I meant it. It was really a miracle that Emma was alright.

A rueful smile crossed her face before she started, "I wasn't. Not at first. I almost lost the ability to walk and did you know what was the first thing my mother said to me when I was awake from the surgery? She said 'It's a pity that she has scars, that modelling career is gone now.' And the next thing she said was to tell me to get plastic surgery."

I watched and listened in silence as she began fidgeting on the couch and hugged her legs to her chest first before continuing. "I went into depression for a year and Theo, my brother - my only family member - supported me along with Zach. My parents did nothing but soak up the attention that I had gained from my accident. And that was when I knew, I had to leave Hollywood."

Good god, was she crying? Shit, I didn't do too well with crying females. Or anyone that was crying. But I couldn't deny it, I recognised that Emma was trying to fight off her tears as she continued. It really must hurt explaining everything. Quickly, I pulled her to me gently and hugged her in my arms as I interjected, "You don't have to tell me-"

She began shaking her head and avoided looking at me, "No, I should. I owe you an explanation. After all, you should have known before we got together."

"Alright, only if you want to tell me," I said quietly and rubbed soothing patterns on her thigh as she leant onto me. "After I realised that I wanted out, my parents disowned me." At that, I tightened my arms around her and she took a deep breath before continuing, "It's safe to say, I don't have parents now and Theo along with Zach had supported me with every decision I had made. Anyway, I had gotten a scholarship in university and here I am today."

I stayed silent, absorbing everything she had told me and I was stunned to hear that her parents didn't want to accept someone like Emma in their life. Finally, I offered softly, "I'm sorry that all this had happened to you."

Emma shook her head and I shifted her so that I could look at her. "It's okay. I'm used to it." Those very words sent something sharp towards my heart and I realised how alone Emma felt. "Well, now you have me too," I said, trying to show that I would be here for her always.

Emma stared up at me stunned as if she couldn't believe what she was hearing. "Thank you for listening to me."

I grinned down at her and tucked a stray curl behind her ear, "Of course, I'm your boyfriend aren't I? That's what we do for our girlfriends."

Suddenly, she blurted out, "I think we shouldn't be together."

Immediately, I froze and frowned, panicked. "What? Why not?"

Emma looked close to tears again and I was alarmed. Had I said the wrong thing? "Because you don't deserve to be stuck with someone like me-"

"Someone like you? Do you mean brilliant? Funny? Absolutely breathtaking?" What the hell was she talking about?

My grip on her tightened as she almost shouted at me, "I can't give you what you want Jack!" I furrowed my brows as I tried to figure out what she meant. "What are you talking about? To me you're perfect."

Suddenly, the tears started rolling down her pale cheeks as she said quietly, "I can't give you children Jack."

"What?" She couldn't mean what she said, could she?

"The accident also took away the ability for me to have children." She repeated blandly and a roaring sound rang through my ears. It sounded as if I was standing near a waterfall and all I could hear was the roar of the water thundering down the rocks.

Sure, I've always thought that I'll - eventually - settle down and have children of my own but this particular situation made me re-evaluate everything. If I could either have children or Emma, I'll choose Emma every time.

"I know you well Jack, at some point in your life, you'll want to have children on your own. I've seen you with your niece and nephews and not to mention Ella. And I can't give them to you and later, you'll start to resent me for it and I can't dea-"

Emma was now talking so fast and I could barely catch what she was saying until I covered her mouth with my hand, "Listen, it doesn't matter to me," I paused when I saw her face and gave her a narrowed stare, "don't assume how I would feel in the future. I have enough niece and nephews with more coming from Gwennie and Emmett and there are other options like adoptions. All I know is that I want you. Children or not."

"But-"

"No buts, I mean it. I want you Emma or Emmaline. But I'll think I'll stick with Em - it's shorter."

She snorted and I hugged her tightly before saying softly, I really do. I told you earlier, you're my dream girl."

Emma stared at me with wide eyes, her cheeks were wet with her tears, "Why do you call me that?"

I could feel a dull flush creep up onto my neck but I offered her a wide grin, You're brilliant, funny, gorgeous and you have that dry sense of humour and not to mention you keep me grounded. You balance me out, when I'm all goofy and full of nonsense, you're serious and practical,"

I was barely done when Emma threw her arms around me and hugged me tightly. Surprised but nonetheless pleased, I pressed a kiss on the top of her head, marvelling at the way her body fit perfectly against mine.

Without thinking, I blurted out, "And now I don't have to wear condoms." Immediately, I could feel myself turn red while Emma snorted and smacked me on the chest, "Don't be an idiot." At that, I couldn't help but laugh but I realised that Emma hadn't really divulged how the accident started.

Briefly, I wondered if it was a good idea to bring that up but curiosity won and I asked hesitantly, "If it's okay to ask...what caused the accident?"

Emma stiffened in my arms and I hastily added, "It's okay if you don't want to say..." Emma shook her head before starting dully and I noted that her face was blank. "I was at a party and I caught my then boyfriend cheating and I told him that I was going to break up with him. He didn't like that and it didn't help he had been drinking heavily. He dragged me to his car and started driving and he got angrier and angrier when I refused to cooperate and that is how the accident happened."

I blinked before feeling that unexplainable rage I had felt earlier and I quickly fought to repress it. Just because of that idiot, Emma had gotten hurt and it wasn't even her fault.

"What a dick," I gritted through my teeth and she shrugged, "It's in the past and I don't really want to talk much about it." I nodded and watched her carefully before asking, "We're still okay right?" I had to know. I couldn't leave with her not with me.

"Yes, if you'll have me," she replied softly and relief so immense swept through me like a tidal wave.

"Good and yes, I'll still have you." With that, I swooped down and kissed her. Slowly, I pulled away and she rested her head on my shoulder. Right there and then, I've never felt as contented before in my life. It felt like all the pieces in my life had finally fit. Looking down, an affectionate smile crossed my face at the sight of Emma almost dozing off.

Making the slight move to leave, her hand tugged lightly on the hem of my shirt. "Stay," she called out drowsily.

"Alright," I replied and pressed another kiss on her forehead before shifting on the couch to get into a more comfortable position and with Emma in my arms, I drifted off to sleep with the fact that everything in my life was perfect now.

* * *

A/N: Interesting fact: this chapter was never meant to happen but because some of you were curious how Jack reacted, here it is. All in his point of view! Anyway, I hope that you guys liked it and please vote and comment and tell me what you all thought? Love you all and thanks so much for reading! <3

Chapter 21-The Apology

Chapter 21-The Apology

Emmaline Heywood's POV

As I sat on my desk, I quickly filed away all the paperwork before reaching for a new folder regarding the replacement of some pieces in the museum for repair and maintenance and my eyes stopped at the picture of Ella and I. That had been there only recently when I felt that I didn't want my office to seem too impersonal.

In the picture, Ella was grinning toothily and I was a little amused that she wanted to show off to the camera that she had an ice-cream in her hand. This had been taken last year and after a month she had given Ella to me.

Now that I had Ella in my life, I couldn't imagine life without her and now, all I wanted more than anything else was for Theo to wake up to meet his incredible daughter and also for Ella to know her father - someone who would love her unconditionally, besides me, unlike her mother.

Also, I was still waiting for the shoe to drop.

I still couldn't wrap my head around the fact that Jack still wanted me despite everything. I was nothing special and I couldn't give him children.

Sure I knew and wanted to have my own at some point in my life. When I was probably thirty or so but at sixteen, that choice was ripped from me and I had to deal with it. I had gotten over it of course but at times, I still longed for it no matter how much I knew that reality was cruel.

Hence, I couldn't even believe why Jack still wanted me. I knew him and seeing him with his nephews and niece, I knew that he would have children and he would be a fantastic dad unlike mine. It wasn't fair to him that he couldn't have any because of me.

However, I was selfish.

No matter how much I knew it would be better for Jack to be without me, I couldn't let him go.

He made me smile and laugh and his personality was a counterpart of my more serious and cynical side. He was the very few people in my life who could make me smile other than Zach and Theo along with Ella.

I couldn't explain the fact that whenever he was around, I couldn't help but brighten up. It was silly and strange and odd but...I liked it.

A smile graced my lips at that and I gradually turned back to the files on my desk. There was work to be done and I really shouldn't spend more time thinking about my life. With a soft sigh, I began looking through the papers about the upcoming exhibition from Greece.

Time must have passed and it wasn't till a soft knock on my door alerted me. Calling out for the person to come in, I was met with the sight of Isadora standing at the doorway with a blank expression on her face.

"Isadora," I greeted tonelessly but a tad surprised as the dark haired woman stepped into my office carefully. "How may I help you?" I questioned a little warily. I didn't dislike Jack's sister-in-law, I just had slight reservations against her.

While I didn't appreciate her announcing everything about me outright, I was a little thankful that she did. Because I knew that I would have never told Jack about it if it were up to me and for that, I was grateful to her for that.

Isadora stared at me before she straightened her back and tilted her chin outwardly, "I came here to..." she hesitated and paused before continuing, "apologise."

From her stance, I could see that the woman wasn't one who apologise or did so often. "Oh?" I eyed her a little cautiously and wondered if anyone - including Jack - had put her up to it.

"Yes, I apologise for the way I had announced your history or secret whichever it is. It wasn't my place to say them and for that I apologise. It was really unkind and insensitive of me to mention things about your brother as well," she said quietly with her gaze levelled with mine.

I gave her a curt nod, my heart clenching at the very mention of the state Theo was in, "I accept your apology. Thank you for coming down to tell me this."

Isadora offered me a tight smile and she shifted on her feet and watching her, she seemed a little hesitant. It was as if she wanted to say something more but she didn't really want to at the same time. Seeing her shift her weight from one feet to the other, the realisation that she was pregnant snapped back to me. "Would you want to take a seat?"

Isadora nodded and strode towards one of the chairs before seating herself gracefully. "I just wanted to let you know my reasons on why I announced it that way. I had thought you were using Jack when I found out and well, I protect my family."

"I understand."

"I know the Donnahue family aren't my immediate family but they're the only family I have," she paused and I waited patiently for whatever she was going to say. From the look on Isadora's face, I could see that whatever she wanted to say was something sensitive and she was looking for the right words to say it.

"While growing up, I was an orphan and I grew up in the orphanage. My parents died due to an accident caused by a drug user. I didn't have any family members to speak of until I met Strider in college. When he married me, I suddenly had people that looked out for me, people that cared about me and well, I didn't know how that felt like until then," Isadora paused and swallowed harshly as if she hated talking about this but I was enthralled with the news that she was sharing.

Never had I thought that the strong confident woman in front of me was someone who grew up without family and I understood a little of psychology, and the strong confident persona Isadora had was a way for her to deal with her insecurities about being alone. And also, her being an orphan due to an accident caused by a drug dealer did make sense about the way she had brought up Theo.

I remained silent and waited for her to continue and I was hoping that my face didn't show any expression of sympathy or pity because I knew that the woman opposite me would resent it.

"The Donnahue family welcomed me into their family despite me being a nobody and that was why I got really upset when I found out your actual identity. I had thought you were using Jack for his fame and money and anyway, I'm sorry that I had judged you based on your past and that

I caused problems between you and Jack. I just hope that you would understand why I had done it and know that I sincerely regret it." Isadora finished and pressed her lips into a thin line with her eyes fixed on mine as if she was trying to defend herself from any pity I would give her.

Watching her, I nodded before replying quietly, "I understand. My parents disowned me for leaving Hollywood when I was sixteen. My brother Theo and Zach supported me ever since."

A look of understanding flashed through Isadora's eyes before she gave me a short nod and the hesitant and uncomfortable expression on her face was gone and was replaced with the usual haughty stare she had on.

Isadora started clearing her throat as she stood up on her two feet before announcing nonchalantly, "Well now that this all done, I'm leaving and I'll let Jack know that I apologised because he ripped me a new arsehole that day when you left that day."

I raised an eyebrow at that and let a small smile tug up on the corner of my mouth, "I see. I wasn't one to peg you to listen to Jack."

Isadora snorted and now that she was back in her comfort zone, she was back to her usual self. "Well, I let him think that he can order me around. But Strider and I know better. Actually, everyone knows better except for Jack."

She slung her bag over her shoulder before tossing her dark hair behind her shoulders and gave me an acknowledging nod, "I'll see you around Emma." And with that, she stalked out of her one inch heels and I blinked before shaking my head.

Well, that was...strange and unexpected, I mused.

Shaking my head, I turned back to my folders but found that I couldn't really concentrate after that bombshell had been dropped onto me by Isadora.

I didn't hold any grudges against her, she was just trying to protect her family and I understood that. I was protecting Ella and I by lying to almost everyone we knew. Hence, I wouldn't fault Isadora for doing so. We may not have done things appropriately to protect our family but that had been our intention.

I gazed at the papers on my desk, the words swimming in my eyes. No matter how hard I tried, I couldn't seem to focus on the words. Too much was on my mind and well - I was distracted.

Another knock on the door sounded and without looking, I demanded, "What?"

"Can't I just drop by to say hello?"

My head snapped up at that teasing tone of his and I gave him a flat stare while trying to fight off the emerging smile on my face. "What are you doing here? You can't just drop by whenever you like."

"It's a pity that my girlfriend doesn't seem pleased to see me especially when I got frozen yoghurt for her but oh, well. Maybe I would give it to the receptionist who always stares at me like I'm fresh meat-"

"Oh hush! I'm just really busy and yes, I appreciate you coming over to give me some frozen yoghurt," I said with a small smile on my face while trying to appear stern.

Jack smirked at me and passed me the cup of frozen goodness before shifting his sunglasses to rest on his head. "Why are you so busy?" he asked as he settled himself on one of the chairs and ate a spoonful of his own yoghurt.

I stared down at my cup and my gaze was stuck on the mountains of rainbow sprinkles on the yoghurt. I didn't like sprinkles, but sneaking a quick glance at jack, I forced myself to smile and eat it slowly.

"There's upcoming exhibitions," I answered and swallowed the mouthful of yoghurt with the millions of sprinkles with great difficulty. God this was worse than dealing with Ella on her sulky days - not that she had many of those thank god.

"Did you know Isadora came by earlier?" I questioned.

A frown crossed his face and he scowled, "What did she want?" He demanded, "Did she come here accusing you again?"

My eyes widened for just a second and I rushed to quickly soothe his sudden anger. "No. She actually came to apologise about her outburst that day."

"She apologised?" Jack echoed, an expression of disbelief on his handsome face.

"Yes and I thank you for coming to my defence that day - she told me about that and once again I thank you. But I understood her reasoning and now all is well between her and I."

I forced another mouthful of yoghurt into my mouth and I wondered if it was possible to scrape off the sprinkles but gave up once I realised the amount of sprinkles there was in the cup before returning my attention to Jack who stared at me with astonishment.

"How can you just forget all about it already? She said awful things about your brother and accused you," Jack demanded and set his cup onto my desk before crossing his arms over his chest.

I refused - simply refused - to admire how his biceps tightened at that action and forced my gaze to meet his as I replied. "I understood her and she and I are not that different. She was trying to protect her family. I lied to you and a lot of people to protect Ella and I."

"But-" he started.

"But nothing. Everything is under the bridge." I sneaked another quick glance at him to see that he still looked unbelievably lost. "Well, you've been rash and impulsive while I'm slower to anger. I complement you don't I? So forget about. I'm over it," I said before swallowing another mouthful of yoghurt and this time, I had managed to eat it without any of the sprinkles.

That was like a victory for me.

Jack stared at me with narrowed eyes before relenting. "Fine. But if Isadora says another thing out of line, she better watch out," he warned and I reached out for his hand and grasped it tightly.

"She won't," I reassured and rubbed soothing patterns on his hand.

"Good. I won't have her disrespecting you or your brother."

"She won't," I repeated and my phone rang. Turning away, I reached for it and answered, "Hello?"

The person on the other line relayed a message to me and I froze.

At the news I had just received, everything seemed to stop as if time was frozen and I couldn't believe what I had just heard. In front of me, Jack was peering at me with his brown eyes that were filled with curiosity as he tried to read the expression on my face to determine if what I was hearing was good news or bad news.

My brother was awake.

* * *

A/N: Hello lovelies! Hope you enjoyed this chapter and please vote and comment and let me know what you think? Thank you so much for reading and I love you all! <3

Chapter 22-The Brother

Chapter 22-The Brother

Emmaline Heywood's POV

My brother was awake.

My brother was awake.

My brother was awake.

That was the only thought that ran on a loop in my mind since I had gotten the news. It was one thing to hope and wish and pray for it but it was another thing for it to actually come true.

I could feel Jack giving me quick glances as he drove us to the hospital. After getting the news from the hospital, I had gone into shock and Jack had taken the phone away from me and decided I wasn't in the right state of mind to be driving anywhere. Hence, he became the driver.

I had thoughts of bringing Ella but I needed to see the condition my brother was in. I had read cases where patients had lost their memories or weren't dealing well with coming out of a coma. I didn't want to give Theo the news of having a daughter when he had so much other things to adapt to.

I was thankful that Jack hadn't spoken but instead led me towards the car and began driving. I didn't know what to say, I didn't even think of a word and don't even bring up stringing a sentence together.

Once Jack had arrived at the hospital, it was a wordless agreement that I head up first while he found a space to park the car and get his disguise on.

The thoughts must have been rushing throughout my head from the minute I entered the hospital till I reached Theo's room. Giving a slight knock against the door, I took a deep breath an entered the room.

The minute I stepped in, my eyes automatically landed on the figure sitting up on the bed with a doctor at his side. It was true. Theo was awake.

Theo looked away from the doctor and gazed at me with wide eyes. "Emmy."

Now that my brother was awake and was sitting up, it was clear that he was more gaunt and pale, his brown eyes were staring at me in disbelief. It was probably due to the fact that he had received the news of being in a coma for more than a year.

Immediately, I could feel the telltale signs of tears coming and I quickly glanced away from him and gave my full attention to the doctor who was waiting patiently - no doubt he was used to all of this.

"Miss Heywood I presume?"

I nodded and the doctor peered at me through his round glasses before doling out my brother's condition and that he was perfectly fine but weak due to the lack of any muscle activity and that it is recommended he stay in the hospital for about a week more for further observation.

I must have given some sign of acknowledgement because the doctor gave me a short curt nod before leaving the room to both Theo and I.

"Emmy," my brother started hoarsely as he stared at me.

I couldn't say anything. Perhaps it was more likely that I didn't know what to say. I was stunned into speechlessness. The news I had received an hour earlier didn't seem real but seeing my brother awake and staring at me and talking to me made everything into a reality.

All the anger and frustration and not to mention the hurt from these past few months of seeing my brother on the verge of death welled up in me.

"You bloody idiot," I hissed through clenched teeth.

"Emmy, I-" Theo started. However I cut him off, "How dare you. Doing drugs! What the hell were you thinking?" I questioned harshly, my tone was so sharp that it could probably cut glass as I repressed the urge to smack him in the head repeatedly. How stupid could you be to turn to drugs just because you felt life was going downhill?

You almost died! You almost left me all alone with Ella. You nearly robbed Ella the chance to meet her father; someone who would love and cherish her the way she should have been from the start.

These were the words I wanted to scream at him but I held them back. It wouldn't be any good to say them now since I was on the verge of breaking down. The emotions were overwhelming me and I couldn't seem to decide what to do first.

I wanted to hug him and ensure it to myself that my brother was alive and well despite him being in the clutches of death for almost a year. I wanted to tell him that I missed him and that I cared for him and that I- I also wanted to rage at him. I wanted to hit him for being stupid enough to turn to drugs because he felt stressed up.

When people were stressed, they either chose to exercise or take a break. Not fucking do drugs that could potentially kill them! Especially the fact that my brother could lose the chance of having a proper relationship with his daughter.

I pressed my lips into a thin line before shaking my head while avoiding my brother's pleading eyes and left the room quietly before these conflicting thoughts escaped my mouth.

Outside, I leaned against the wall and slumped down onto the ground. I had never thought that my brother would wake after all these months accompanied with discouraging news and updates from the hospital staff. But now that he was, I didn't know how to behave or decide on what to say.

It was ridiculous seeing that he was my brother - my twin. I should be glad that he's alright - which I was - but all those feelings I had when I first found out that he had almost died struggled furiously to be expressed.

I was ecstatic that my brother was okay. He was lucid and there didn't seem to be anything wrong with him. It was just the shock and relief overwhelming me at the moment.

"Hey, what are you doing? Shouldn't you be inside? Unless...there's something wrong?" Jack crouched down in front of me and reached out to tilt my head up, "Are you okay?"

I gave jerky nods, "I'm fine. I just- Now that Theo is really awake and he's fine, I- I don't what to say..." I trailed off and hugged myself tightly, the threat of tears was near and Jack pulled me into his arms and squeezed me comfortingly.

"I get it, but I'm here for you. Do you want to stay out here longer or do you want to go back in?" He pulled back slightly and looked down at me, concern in those brown eyes of his. I nodded and blinked the tears back, "Yes, I just have so many things to say. I'm glad that he's alright but angry at him for turning to drugs and I have to let him know that he has a daughter and-"

"And we'll take things one step at a time. Don't worry and don't stress out. I'm here for you." Jack interjected and gave me a reassuring grin while his thumb caressed my cheek gently.

I drew a shaky breath. "Alright." With that, I pulled away from Jack and entered the room once more. A nurse had appeared in the room and was attending to Theo before leaving after recording something down on a clipboard.

"Emmy please," Theo started once more and I slowly walked towards him. Getting no response from me, my brother tried again, "Emmaline-"

I ignored him before pulling him in for a hug. Automatically, he hugged me back and I leaned my chin on his shoulder while the tears I had fought back escaped and rolled down my cheeks. I must have made some gasping sound because Theo hugged me tighter and we stayed that way for quite some time.

Shuddering, I squeezed my eyes shut and exhaled shakily as I burrowed my face into his neck.

I had my brother back.

* * *

It was sometime later that we realised that we both crying and had snot and tears on each other. Quickly pulling away, I let out a laugh before wiping the tears away with the back of my hand.

Settling onto the seat beside the bed, I looked at my brother before breaking into a small smile, "You're really back."

Theo nodded and ran his hands through his shoulder length hair before giving me a wan smile. "Yeah. A year. I- It just felt like yesterday. God, I have to cut this," he grumbled as he tugged at his hair.

Just hearing his nonchalance about it made all the anger simmer again. Sure, I knew Theo was probably having his regrets but the fact that he could talk about it so easily made me want to snap at him. Yes, he may have suffered but so had I.

It was hell for me the entire time Theo had been in a coma. I had to live with the very fact that he may never wake up and the guilt I felt about it was like poison sinking into my veins, killing me slowly.

I was his twin, his older sister, albeit by two minutes. Hence, he was my younger brother. I should have been looking out for him. I should've seen the signs. I could have prevented it all. But I hadn't. What kind of older sister was I? Theo only had me and Ella - not that he knew about her - but it was the same principle.

And just hearing how casual he was about it made me so angry. He didn't know about the nights I spent crying or how much I resented myself for not looking out for him.

"Why? Why did you turn to drugs?" I demanded in a harsh tone while I made sure to keep my face blank from any expression.

Theo stared at me, stunned from my outburst as he gaped at me like an unattractive goldfish. His mouth working as he tried to think of a reply. "Emmy, I- I don't have a good reason. Or more specifically, I don't have a reason you would consider hearing."

"Why?" I repeated.

Theo stared at me before looking away as he began to speak quietly, "It felt like I didn't have a purpose anymore, acting was fun but it didn't bring that sense of fulfilment or achievement any longer and I got so sick of having that loss that I turned to drugs."

I shook my head in disbelief and looked down at the ground. "Did you know what your actions have done? I blame myself for the state you were in. I'm your older sister! I should've realised that something was wrong. Did you even think about the consequences? Did you even realise how I would feel? You're all I had and if you died - which you almost did, I would be all alone!"

Theo stared at me, his face full of guilt and shame as he tried to reach out to me. "Emmy, I know I was foolish and stupid and I know I shouldn't have done drugs and I'm sorry. I'm sorry for making you worry and putting you into that position," he offered softly and looked away from me.

The hospital clothes he was wearing hung onto his thin frame making it more apparent that he had lost a lot of weight. Theo hung his head and stared at the stark white top he had on before looking up at me. His brown eyes met mine and I could see all the repentance and shame in them.

"I'm sorry Emmaline, I wasn't thinking."

"Did you know what your actions could have done to me? To Ella? What if you had died?" I questioned flatly as I crossed my arms and glanced away from him.

"Who's Ella?"

"Your daughter!"

All the colour in my brother's face drained and I took some sick satisfaction from it. God I really was horrid. "What? Daughter? I-"

"Yes, daughter. She's five this year," I interrupted.

Theo stared at me as if he was checking if I was pulling his leg and when he realised that I was dead serious, I could see that he was mentally counting down the years.

"How did I not know about her?" he demanded and his eyes narrowed. "Her mother is Willa right?"

Hearing that witch's name, I scoffed, "Yes. Apparently, that stupid cow didn't tell you about Ella until you got into a coma. Ella was four when her mother passed her to me."

Theo blinked and stared at me blankly as he digested everything slowly. "I know it's a lot to take in but-"

"Do you have a photo of her?" Theo ran his hands through his hair nervously and at that moment, I realised that my brother wasn't that shocked about finding out that he was a dad but more of the fact that he didn't know how to be one.

"Her name is Ella." I reached out for my bag and fished for my wallet where there was a picture of Ella grinning and took it out and handed it to Theo who stared at it with an expression of utter surprise and reverence.

"She's perfect," Theo breathed out in awe and with what seemed like happiness and I nodded. "She looks like me," Theo commented as he observed Ella's features while tracing her face on the photograph.

"I know. She's a lot like you too."

"Does she know about me?" Theo questioned, his eyes burning with hope and I nodded, "Yeah. She knows about you and how you look like and I explained to her that you were unwell and hence, you're resting in the hospital."

Theo nodded and his attention was once brought back to the photograph of Ella in his hand. "Can I meet her? I know that I must have caused you loads of grief and pain and I can never apologise enough about that but I can meet her?"

I nodded with a small smile, "Of course. She's your daughter. I'll be concerned if you didn't want to meet her."

Theo grimaced and was about to obviously comment on our parent's poor parenting skills when the door cracked open and Jack entered with a bag of potato chips in his hand along with a can of soda in the other. "Is everything alright now?"

I blinked and it was then I realised that the entire time, Jack had not even been in the room. "Where were you? I just realised you weren't even here."

Jack gave me a sheepish grin before gesturing to the snacks in his hand. "I got hungry and before I could enter I could hear shouting and crying and I thought it was better for you to have your reunion with your brother first before I came in."

I snorted and turned back to Theo who was studying Jack with furrowed brows. "You're that actor guy aren't you? That actor who always acts in those cheesy romance movies"

I stifled a laugh and I could see Jack grimacing before he handed me his snacks and went towards my brother and raised a hand for Theo to shake. "Yeah. I guess you can refer to me as that. Anyway, I'm Jack Donnahue."

"Right yes. It's nice to meet you again. But what are you doing here?" Theo questioned and his eyes darted between Jack and I suspiciously.

I glanced up at Jack who in turn looked at me for guidance on how to broach this topic. Turning to Theo, I stated casually, "He's my boyfriend."

Theo looked at me and then at Jack and then back at me before nodding his head. "Oh. Alright. I see. Well uhm. That's great," Theo mumbled awkwardly and I raised an eyebrow before letting a smile cross my face. "At least that hasn't changed," I commented with amusement.

Theo made a face before peering at me hopefully, "So I can meet Ella?"

I glanced at my watch and coincidentally, it was almost time for me to pick Ella up from kindergarten. "Yeah, I can go fetch her now. Kindergarten just ended."

Theo looked both excited and yet nervous at the same time and he nodded eagerly. "Yeah. That's uh okay."

I got to my feet and leaned down to press another kiss on Theo's cheek. "I'm glad that you're okay," I murmured softly and Theo gave me a rueful smile, "Me too."

Turning to leave, I gestured for Jack to come with me but Theo interjected, "Its' alright. Jack can stay and keep me company won't you?"

I rolled my eyes, I should have known that Theo was going to pull the protective brother crap and I obviously knew better to get involved in this. I shot a glance to Jack who reassured me that it was fine, "It's alright. We can trade acting stories with each other."

"Right." I hefted my bag over my shoulder before shooting Theo a stern look to behave, "I'll be back in at most thirty minutes. Try not to kill each other over your 'acting stories' will you?"

Theo shook his head before waving me off, "Don't worry, the most we'll be doing is fake throwing punches at each other."

Jack gave me a look full of panic and I rolled my eyes before exiting the room. It was only when the door was shut that I allowed a wide smile to cross my face.

I really had my brother back.

* * *

A/N: Hello! I hope that the reunion between Emma and Theo has met your expectations or exceeded them ;) Let me know your thoughts on Theo's character? I always liked reading them! Also don't forget to vote and comment! Thank you all so much for reading and I love you all so much! <3

Chapter 23-The Interrogation

Chapter 23-The Interrogation

Jack Donnahue's POV

"So..." I started before trailing off awkwardly. Why the hell had I agreed to stay behind and not go with Emma to get Ella from kindergarten? What the hell was I thinking? I really must have been drinking too much coffee.

Emma's brother, Theo stared at me scrutinisingly and shifted on the hospital bed. "How did you meet my sister? From what I remember - which is a year ago - she didn't seem too keen on dating."

Settling onto the couch at the end of the room which was positioned opposite the bed, I met his gaze evenly and replied awkwardly, "Ha, uh, that's a long story," I paused and reached out to scratch my head nervously. "I bumped into Emma and she didn't like me and I chased after her, we became friends and yeah..." I finished and trailed off.

"I see," Theo said, his head nodding in understanding as he leaned back on the bed, a contemplative expression on his face as he took in my words.

"Do tell me about yourself," Theo requested as he stared at me.

It was odd. This man was about four years younger than me but he was already commanding respect and I admired that about him for looking out for Emma. It was good that she had someone - probably multiple someones - that cared and worried about her.

I cleared my throat before starting, I was determined to make a good impression on Theo, he was Emma's brother and only family - besides Ella, but she didn't really count.

"I'm the middle child. I have two older brothers and one younger sister and brother. My mother passed away when I was young, in fact I don't remember her at all. My dad? I have no idea where he actually. I'm originally from Boston and uh, I started acting when I turned twenty, before I was in college trying to major in science but well, I dropped out. And yeah..."

Theo nodded, looking thoughtful and curious at the same time as if he wanted to ask me something but changed his mind halfway and a sombre atmosphere entered the room.

"You know even though we don't have parents, Emmaline still has people that look out for her. I'm sure you must have met Zach, her best friend from young, he may be a geek to you, but he used to be on the football team in college, in fact he was the captain of the team if memory serves me right," Theo said, the serious and solemn expression on his face contradicting the light conversational tone his voice was using. "All those gym sessions must have been exhausting. I heard it was a daily thing."

I nodded my head and kept silent. Zachary Richmond used to play football? That was news. Theo added, "And well, even though I'm younger than Emmaline, I still look out for her. She has been through things that no one should and I make the effort to try to protect her." Theo narrowed his eyes at me. "You do know what she has been through do you?"

"Yes, the accident and everything with it like the results. Emma did tell me," I said quickly, hoping to reassure Theo who looked quite worried as if he spilled Emma's secret.

"Right." Theo looked quite relieved before it was masked and his demeanour turned serious once more. "Well, not to mention my bodyguard who quite adores Emmaline and sees her like another daughter. Well, I'm sure you get the picture."

I nodded my head and tried to convey how sincere I was. "I am. I'm glad that Emma has people looking out for her and I promise that I would never hurt her." I promised seriously and I guessed Theo must have been convinced because the serious atmosphere in the room left and I could feel myself relax marginally.

"Good. Oh! One more thing, I'm sure you know I have connections and influence even though I'm younger than you. Hurt my sister and I'll make sure you get run out of Hollywood." For someone who was making threats, Theo Heywood didn't appear like he was with that award-winning smile on his face.

I got to my feet and made my way towards the bed before giving my hand for him to shake, "I assure you, Emma's happiness is my priority goal."

Theo narrowed his eyes at me before taking my hand and shook it. For a man who just got out of a coma, he really did have a strong grip, I mused. "Good, that's all I wanted for her."

Stupidly and - obviously - without thinking, I blurted out, "I think I'm in love her."

Shit, what the hell?! That wasn't something I wanted to say to anyone! Especially not with Emma's brother! I wanted to take those words back! I didn't mean to say them! What the hell was I thinking?! Obviously being in a hospital wasn't good for me. No doubt those sedatives given to patients must be floating in the air and I must have inhaled them.

Shit! I was panicking inwardly but on the outside, I was sure that I looked sick from that admission. What if Theo told Emma? God, that would ruin everything! Goddamn it!

Theo looked stunned at my confession but nonetheless surprised but pleased. "Really? Does my sister know?" he questioned as he leaned back onto the bed that was inclined.

I kept silent and shook my head, feeling stupid and embarrassed and from how hot I was feeling, I knew I was flushing from mortification. Maybe Gwennie was right, I was a teenage girl in a thirty-year old male body.

"Ah, well. That can be a secret between us then." Theo flashed me a reassuring smile and ran his hands through his hair and glanced at the clock before turning back to me. A slightly worried expression was on his face.

"Have you met her?"

I raised an eyebrow and for a moment, I was confused. Who was Theo talking about? And then it hit me. Theo was referring to Ella and it didn't take a genius to see that he was anxious and nervous about meeting his daughter.

I nodded and immediately grinned at the thought of the little blonde girl, "Yeah, she's brilliant. Emma did a fantastic job raising Ella."

"What is she like? What does she like and dislike?" Theo seemed frantic for me to answer and I guessed the nerves were getting him which wasn't a surprise. Hell, if I had a daughter I just knew about, I would be nervous as well.

"Funnily, Ella actually likes vegetables which is pretty weird. She loves raspberries - anything to do with them. In fact, she loves all kinds of sweets with the exception of liquorice. She really doesn't like it when there's sprinkles in her ice-cream - which is weird as well seeing that Emma likes them."

Theo stared at me, clearly surprised before he stated, "Emma hates sprinkles."

That caused me to frown. "What? No, she likes them. I gave her frozen yoghurt with sprinkles and she likes them."

"No," Theo said slowly. "She doesn't."

I blinked but before I could respond, a knock sounded on the door and Emma opened it cautiously as if she was afraid to find two dead bodies in the room.

Theo froze and his eyes landed on the small figure of Ella hiding behind Emma's legs. Emma stepped into the room and Ella entered slowly, her big brown eyes taking in everyone in the room. The minute she caught sight of me, her little face brightened up. "Jack!"

Immediately, a wide smile crossed my face, "La La! How is Miss Unicorn and Miss Marissa?" I questioned seriously and Ella beamed, happy that I remembered, "Emma says they need loads of rest!"

"I see, I hope that they will recover soon, remember to feed them with loads of sprinkles and honey." At the very mention of sprinkles, Ella frowned and I sneaked a look at Emma to see her grimacing as well.

Fine, sprinkle haters.

Emma cleared her throat and Ella's gaze turned towards Theo and she became shy and hid behind Emma's legs once more while peeking at Theo. The expression on Theo's face was one I would never forget. He was frozen and speechless as he stared at Ella. A look of adoration and awe was plastered on his face as if he couldn't believe what he was seeing.

Silently, I strode further away from the bed and to the opposite end of the room where I wouldn't interrupt. This was a Heywood family thing after all.

"Ella," Emma started softly as she held the girl's hand gently and led her towards the bed. "This is Theo, your dad."

Ella shyly said, "Hi."

Theo seemed befuddled and he croaked out, "Hi." Then silence reigned in the room before Ella questioned curiously, "Do you like unicorns?"

Theo stared at her as if he was frozen before he enthusiastically nodded his head, "Yes, the pink ones are my favourite." With that, Ella came up out of her shell. "Really? Those are my favourite too!"

And the rest was history. Ella started babbling and even though I knew her far longer than Theo, I was still surprised by her ability to talk for so long without even stopping for breath.

My gaze turned towards Emma who was standing nearby the pair and was watching them with a smile on her face and what seemed like happy tears in her eyes. Theo was enraptured by Ella and he seemed more stunned as he took in the sight of his daughter talking to him without any reservations.

Ella on the other hand, didn't seem shocked or anything like her dad. In fact, there was a sparkle in her brown eyes. Eyes that she shared with Theo. Now that they were side by side (sort of), I could really see the resemblance between them.

Other than Theo's light brown eyes, Ella seemed to share his facial features, the dimples, the high forehead, the sharp cheekbones (that were covered by baby fat) and the heartbreaking smile. Her face was rounder than Theo's but I was sure that she would resemble Theo way more than her mother.

I knew who was Ella's mother of course. I've never met her but I knew of her. It was easy to say that she wasn't a very nice person to begin with. But after hearing what she had done with Ella, I had little to no respect for her.

To deny someone's child from them and then discard her own daughter as if she was a piece of used tissue was ridiculously horrid. I knew Emma resented her. In fact, I was pretty sure if my girlfriend saw that woman again, a fight would ensue. Not a screaming match of course, a physical one. And I was pretty sure Emma would win.

"And then, the fairies would have made Miss Unicorn very upset if Mrs Sparkly didn't help her find her present." Ella was now on the bed facing Theo with a very serious expression on her face. Theo was gazing down at her with a wide smile on his face and I could see that he adored her.

Well, who wouldn't?

I guess I must have been too busy staring at the father-daughter reunion that I didn't notice Emma sidling up beside me until she sat down.

I turned to her and she leaned against me, exhaustion in her features but no one could deny that she was extremely happy that Theo was awake. "You okay?"

Emma nodded, "Yeah. I'm just overwhelmed and Ella finally gets to meet her dad." She started tearing up and laughed, "I'm sorry for being so emotional."

"It's fine. I'm glad too. Theo seems like he's going to be a great dad." I grinned and wrapped an arm over her shoulders as we both gazed at the scene of Theo and Ella drawing on a piece of paper.

Emma laughs softly and she turns to face me, "So, I hope that during your 'fake punching sessions' didn't result into anyone being actually punched."

"Of course not. We just had a discussion about football," I lied and Emma raised an eyebrow skeptically. "Right," she said but didn't push for more.

Suddenly remembering something crucial, I poked her in the rib and she jumped and shot me a little glare, "Ow. What was that for?"

"Do you or do you not hate sprinkles?"

Emma blinked and frowned, "What?"

"Do you or do you not hate sprinkles?" I repeated, a stern expression on my face and Emma rolled her eyes. "No, I don't have a fancy for them."

"Why didn't you tell me earlier when I bought that frozen yoghurt with sprinkles on it?" I demanded and Emma gave me a flat stare. "Because, you already bought it and I didn't want you to waste it."

I waved away her excuses, "That's bullshit, you could have told me that day when I bought you ice-cream or that day when we had dessert or that day when I added sprinkles into your bowl of popcorn."

"You added sprinkles to popcorn?" a disbelieving snort let her mouth as Emma stared at me as if I was mad.

I waved her comment away and hastily added, "That's not important. Why didn't you tell me you didn't like sprinkles?"

Emma narrowed her eyes and remained silent as she tilted her chin stubbornly and I knew she wasn't going to say anything else on the subject.

Brightening up, I gave her a cheeky grin, "Unless, the reason you didn't say anything is because you didn't want to hurt my feelings?" I wriggled my eyebrows and smirked smugly. In response, Emma sputtered and she seemed to not know what to say.

"I'm right aren't I?"

Emma scowled and crossed her arms over her chest defensively, "I refuse to say anymore on this subject." I let out a low laugh and wrapped an arm around her shoulder, bringing her body closer to mine. "It's okay to be embarrassed to say so. I understand and I promise I would never tell anyone," I said seriously and Emma glared at me and jabbed her fingers at my sides.

"No! If that makes - Eeep" she let out a squeak when I pressed my lips against hers to make her stop talking. At first, Emma struggled to push me away but eventually gave up and kissed me back. Her arms were draped around my neck as she deepened the kiss while my arms held her waist tightly.

We would have continued kissing except for the fact that we had forgotten that Theo and Ella were in the room with us. "Hey! I may be okay with this but I do not want to see anything! I'm not on my death bed yet!"

Emma pulled away from me and shot her brother a glare, "Don't say that you idiot!" Pulling away from my embrace, Emma got to her feet and began fussing over her brother while Ella giggled at the face her father pulled due to it.

Just watching Emma made my insides twist. I felt sick but in a good way, like sweet anticipation. How the hell was I going to tell her that I was in love with her?

* * *

A/N: Hi all! So sorry for the late update! I have no good excuses because I was too caught up with Leigh Bardugo's Six of Crows and catching up on Game of Thrones. I'm sorry, I know! Anyway, I hope that this chapter has met your expectations and that you liked it! Please give a vote and comment and let me know what you guys think?

By the way, I just watched Miss Peregrine's Home for Peculiar Children and shit, it was bloody good. But the book was better. Anyway, thanks so much for reading and I love you all!

Chapter 24-The News

Chapter 24-The News

Emmaline Heywood's POV

"Emmy?"

"Yeah?" I questioned, turning to face my brother while continuing to stroke through Ella's hair as she lay sleeping on me.

"Did you ever... hate me?" Theo questioned, his eyes avoiding mine as they focused on his daughter instead. I blinked and furrowed my brows. "Why would you ask something like that? You're my brother, I can never hate you," I said quietly and reached out to grab his hand.

"You should. I've caused you so much pain and sorrow and Ella deserves someone better than me to look after."

"Theo, it doesn't matter. I forgave you. Of course I'm still mad but all that matters is that you're okay now. Everything will slowly go back to normal - sort of," I reassured my brother who sighed heavily and finally met my earnest gaze. Guilt was swimming in those brown eyes of his and he looked extremely tired.

"I'm sorry Emmy for everything I've put you through. I'm a rotten brother."

Feeling some form of annoyance creep up on me, I began to scowl a little. "Shut up," I snapped, hoping that I wouldn't wake Ella up. "You're not a horrid brother. You may not be perfect but no one is. You were there for me during the Incident and I have absolutely no idea what would happen if you weren't."

Theo nodded and reached forward to take Ella from me. Seeing the sight of the little girl in his arms made me tear up. Despite Theo waking up two weeks ago, I was still emotional because it felt like a dream. As if it wasn't reality that he was fine and awake and reunited with Ella.

"I'll still have to say I'm so sorry Emm-"

"Shut up. Anymore apologising and I will tape your mouth." I glared and stared at him sternly and Theo chuckled lowly at my response.

Comfortable silence reigned in the room and a thought popped into my head. Theo was being released tomorrow and it has certainly been sheer luck that no one from the hospital had revealed to the press that he was awake. Hence, the lack of reporters.

"Have you sorted out living arrangements? After all, Ella would be back to staying with you eventually." The thought of the five-year-old that brightened up my life leaving my apartment brought a slight ache to my heart which was ridiculous. She wasn't going away, she was just staying with her dad and I could always see her anytime.

Theo scratched his head and shrugged, "I haven't given much thought about it to be honest. I've called the caretaker at my home already and well

I think it would be best for Ella to stay with you for a while more until things are settled. She's just known me for two week and you a year." He sighed and continued, "I think its best for her to be more accustomed to me before she stays with me."

A proud smile formed on my face at that. Never would I have thought my brother would have grown up and matured. He was definitely going to be a good dad. "I see. Maybe while you get your lawyers and your housing and career arrangement sorted out, you could always bunk in with me. I have a spare room and it will help you bond with Ella."

Theo nodded and a large smile stretched across his face as he gazed down in adoration at Ella. "Yeah, that sounds great."

My smile faded as I realised something else. "I think its best you settle Ella's custody issues as soon as possible. Once news is spread about you being awake and having a daughter, that attention seeking cow would be back to try to get her away from you," I advised and Theo nodded, grim determination filled his features.

"Yes, you're right. I can get sole custody on the grounds of abandonment. After all, she did abandon Ella by giving her to you."

A short laugh left me as I heard what he said, "Sometimes I wonder what do you even learn from acting and I get my answers when that sort of thing pops out from your mouth."

In response, Theo stuck his tongue out at me.

* * *

Heywood out of coma!

It is reported that Theo Heywood who has been in a coma for about a year due to a drug overdose has recently woken up and is released from the hospital! He has been seen with an entourage of bodyguards while exiting the hospital yesterday looking in good health. An anonymous source has claimed that he has suffered no serious drawbacks.

However parents, reality stars Henry and Adeline Heywood were no where in sight. It is no secret that the Heywood family has had a severe falling out a few years ago. What was surprising was the sight of Heywood's sister Emmaline who was seen beside her brother as they left the hospital together.

What was even more surprising was the sight of Hollywood heartthrob Jack Donnahue present at the scene as well. He was seen standing beside Emmaline Heywood as all of them left together. All this author wants are answers to her many questions. The most important being; What exactly is going on?

Heywood twins have daughter from incest?

It has come to a shock when it was reported that Theo Heywood has had a daughter. The pair were seen together in an ice-cream parlour with a large group of body guards. Speculations have arose that the child could have been the product of incest. Hence the reason why Emmaline Heywood, former model and actress has not been seen in the spotlight six years ago and thus the reason for the Heywood family falling out.

Willa George reveals all!

Model Willa George has sat down for an interview just yesterday revealing the true parentage of Theo Heywood's five-year-old daughter. George, claimed that her brief relationship with Heywood about five years ago have resulted in a pregnancy, which is daughter five-year-old Ella. She has also revealed that Heywood has paid her off to get an abortion to which she has profusely refused.

Since, Heywood has ordered for her not to mention their daughter and has even filed a restraining order against her. When asked to elaborate, George broke down into tears, "He didn't even want her. She is his daughter and he abandoned her! Hence the reason I'm sharing this with everyone! He has to be exposed!"

When asked to comment, Heywood has refused to say anything. He has also implied that George has fabricated the whole story and had no idea about his daughter's existence till this year. He also intends to file for sole custody on the grounds of abandonment.

Heywood wins sole custody!

It has come to no surprise that Theo Heywood has won sole custody for Ella Heywood. The saga between George and Heywood is certainly well known and has even led to fans taking sides. Heywood has revealed in past interviews that it was his sister, Emmaline who has been taking care of Ella the past year while he's been in a coma. The false truth that George has revealed has resulted in more fans taking Heywood's side and is rooting for him to win.

The image on the left shows a triumphant looking Heywood with a scowling George as they exit the courthouse. Ella, on the other hand is with Emmaline Heywood with bodyguards surrounding them. It also didn't escape onlookers' notice that Jack Donnahue is once again at the scene.

This has led to questions being raised about the relationship between the pair. Meanwhile, Heywood has been answering questions regarding his career and his current status, no doubt elated about his win against George.

Heywood has gained sole custody with no visitation rights given to George due to the grounds of abandonment a year ago. Twin sister, Emmaline Heywood has also stepped in to testify as a witness.

Emmaline Heywood back in Hollywood?

Theo Heywood being back in Hollywood since last week has led to more sightings of his sister Emmaline Heywood. Questions are raised if she would be back into the modelling or acting industry.

Emmaline Heywood, 26 was last seen in the Hollywood industry when she was 16 before vanishing after a car accident. Now, she is currently working as a museum director in the state museum.

Speculations have also been formed regarding the nature of the relationship with Hollywood actor Jack Donnahue. That being said, the pair were recently spotted together despite wearing sunglasses to avoid being recognised. It was also noted that Donnahue had been seen around with Heywood at the trial and at the hospital when her brother was released.

Fans are wondering if the pair are officially together seeing that they are no official statements being made. When questioned, Donnahue declined to comment. However, a source has indicated that the pair have been seeing each other for quite a few months now and are considered quite exclusive.

The most recent sighting of the pair were seen together with Heywood's niece and no one could say they didn't make a cute little family. Could this be a sign of something more?

* * *

"I hate reporters! Honestly!" I growled in anger and exasperation as I tossed the stupid magazine away from me and onto the table. "Could they not leave me alone?" I muttered before slouching onto the sofa.

Jack snorted loudly and began impatiently ripping open the popcorn bag. "You'll get used to it," he answered as his voice echoed slightly due to his location in the kitchen.

I pressed my lips into a thin line while getting to my feet and began heading into the kitchen to see Jack pushing the bowl of popcorn into the microwave. "That's extremely easy for you to say. No one accused you of having relations with your siblings," I sneered a little as that particular article popped into my mind.

Jack bit back laughter seeing the foul expression on my face as he handed me two cans of soda and ushered me out of the kitchen. "Ignore them, that's what I do," he added helpfully.

I sighed heavily before placing the two cans of soda onto the coffee table and ran my fingers through my hair. "I just want to be invisible again," I mumbled and Jack shrugged, "But I was sure you were aware of the news when your brother is awake."

"Yes, I just-I was prepared but facing all those reporters screaming their questions at me, stalking me- Did you see that picture of us and Ella having ice-cream in that gossip rag? I wasn't even aware they were around," I complained half-heartedly.

I had been prepared that attention would be on me once Theo was awake. I wasn't going to hide while my brother tried to get his life back in order, I would be there to support him every step of the way just like had done with me in the past. However, I hadn't expected how jarring and annoying the press was.

It was made worse due to the fact that I was always spotted with Jack. I wasn't even aware that my boyfriend was so popular with people. I was just surprised that I hadn't received any hate mail from his hardcore fans.

Hearing the microwave's beeps that alerted us that our popcorn was ready, Jack stood up and went to get it while I shuffled through the DVD stacks hoping that Jack had not brought any of his silly cheesy movies.

"Here we go and no! We are not watching one of your horror nonsense," he cut in and I watched in dismay as he easily slid one of his silly movies into the player before I could object.

Jack gave me a charming smirk from over his shoulder before it morphed into a triumphant smug grin once he caught sight of the expression on my face. "Cheer up Em, maybe next time, you'll be quick enough to choose the movie," he taunted lightly as he sat beside me.

I gave him a playful shove and he chuckled before pulling me into his side, one of his arms were wrapped around my shoulders and I leaned my head against his chest as the DVD began to load.

"Honestly, I still don't see how this is appealing to anyone," I pointed out while Jack huffed and he quickly reached over for the remote once we realised the television wasn't in the DVD player mode.

He was about to switch the channels when a pair of very familiar faces caught my eye on some stupid entertainment channel.

"Wait."

My eyes narrowed as the screen showed my mother gushing and tearing up about the miraculous recovery of Theo and how hurt she felt when neither Theo or I told her about Ella.

I was still surprised that her tear ducts could even work after the many surgeries she went.

My jaw clenched as the reporter turned towards my father who was feigning disappoint and happiness as he expressed joy and sadness about not knowing that he had a granddaughter.

I could feel Jack's eyes on me as he watched me carefully. It was as if he was preparing for me to start screaming or shouting or doing something totally impulsive. However, the only thing I did was snatch the remote out of his hand and changed the channel to the DVD mode.

Awkward silence reigned and thankfully, before Jack could say something, the opening credits of the movie began and I relaxed slightly into him.

The movie was only playing for about ten minutes when Jack paused it and scrutinised me. "Would you want to talk about your parents?"

I scoffed and shook my head, pulling away from him slightly. "No. I don't have parents. You could tell they were faking it right? They never really cared about Theo or me except for fame and money," I bit out and clenched my jaw bitterly.

Jack reached out and pushed back a stray lock of hair behind my ear and gave me a boyish yet shy grin, "Well you got me now." He leaned forward to grab some popcorn and popped it into his mouth.

I allowed a wan smile to form on my face before bowing my head to stare at my hands which were curled up on my lap.

"Sometimes," I started softly, "I wish I could just pack up and leave everything behind. Away from all of this."

Jack seem to freeze for awhile and his smile faded. "Really?"

I nodded slowly, "Yes, like another state or anywhere far away from my parents and Hollywood itself."

Jack blinked and looked away, the corner of his mouth tilted down. "What's wrong?" I asked warily, noting his eyes were avoiding my searching ones.

"Nothing," he quickly feigned a smile and tugged me towards him again. "It's just the popcorn. They're all cold now."

Somehow, I couldn't help but feel that he was lying.

* * *

A/N: Well. I'm sorry this took so long. To be short, I had some trouble figuring out the plot and well I'm pleased to announce that everything will be back on track. Thank you all so much for being patient and supportive and understanding and I love you all! I hope this chapter meets your expectations and please vote and comment? Also, there would be about 5- 6 chapters left for this book and it will be done before 2016 ends. That I can promise!

Chapter 25-The Advice

All Rights Reserved

Chapter 25-The Advice

Emmaline Heywood's POV

A loud sigh broke me out of my thoughts and I darted my gaze up to see Zach scrutinising me. "Alright, what gives?"

"What are you talking about?" I frown and leant against my chair as I stirred my cup of tea.

"Em, I've known you since we were kids and obviously, something's up. You're in a daze and don't bother lying, you're awful at it," Zach questioned lightly as he drummed his fingers on the table.

I turned my head away from those prying eyes that belonged to my best friend and took a quick sip. "It's nothing, just some work issues."

Zach narrowed his eyes as he tilted his head to the right while studying me. "Shut up and stop lying."

"You know just because you're looking at me in a different angle, it doesn't mean it can magically allow you to read my thoughts," I pointed out dryly to which Zach rolled his eyes in response - he was definitely used to my sarcasm by now.

"Avoiding my face is one fact that proves to me that you're lying to me."

"Zach, I just said its a work thing," I said tiredly. "Enough about me, how's the upcoming wedding plans?"

My best friend stared at me for a little while longer, no doubt debating if he should drop the subject or rise to my bait to change the subject.

Fortunately, Zach could tell I wasn't in one of my amicable moods for he went with the latter. "It's alright. Everything is actually going quite smoothly which is very surprising. But in my opinion, I feel that it is because my fiancée is a monster when angered rather than the competence of those establishments."

I nodded my head along with him, silently agreeing. From what I knew of Gwendolyn Donnahue and the past meetings with her, she was a force to be reckoned with and I was never going to tell Zach that I thought that his fiancée was the one who wore the pants in the relationship.

But well, I think Zach would be alright with that. From the way he spoke of her, I knew that he adored every little thing about her despite her rather fear-inspiring temper.

It was exactly like a romantic movie and I couldn't help but admire it. They were one in a million who experienced that and I couldn't be happier for my best friend.

However, the thought of movies especially those with the romance genre made my mood dampen even further.

It reminded me of Jack.

I didn't know why but ever since the news of Theo and I hit the headlines, Jack was more...distant. I couldn't exactly put a finger on where and why but I could feel him slowly drifting away from me.

The smiles he gave me were smaller and a little more strained and he seemed to be a little more guarded around me. His jokes and humour were a little on the forced side and I couldn't help but wonder if this was it.

Was this the moment that he realised it was better to leave when he could since I obviously couldn't give him a family?

Truth be told, deep down, I was still expecting for this to happen and now that it was, I wasn't too surprised. But it still hurt. It hurt like hell. Like a swift punch to the gut followed by a hand squeezing my heart.

I would never admit it but the very thought of Jack leaving did tear me up inside.

"Okay, you're drifting away from me again. What is it? I'm your best friend Em, you should be able to tell me things," Zach's voice snapped me back to the present and I could only blink owlishly at him.

"I meant it when-"

"Em, don't make me pull the truth out of you," Zach interrupted impatiently.

As my response, I stared at him passively, hiding the emotional turmoil. The expression on my face was utterly blank and I liked it that way. Because, if no one could see your emotions, they wouldn't be able to use it against you.

"Good God, how does Jack even deal with you?" Zach questioned exasperatedly as he ran his fingers through his already messy hair.

I couldn't help but flinch a tiny bit at the very mention of his name and thanks to my cursed luck, Zach noticed.

"What did Jack do? Did he hurt you?" Zach demanded, his eyes turning hard at the very image of that.

"No! Of course not!" I snapped in response and threw him a glare. "What the hell are you talking about? He would never do anything like that!"

Zach calmed down a little at that before studying me carefully while I remained mulishly silent.

"Em, I know its hard for you to talk about your feelings. In fact, I actually think it'll be easier to yank out your teeth than for you to say what you're really feeling but holding it won't solve whatever issues you have with Jack."

My eyes darted towards to him, "I didn't say there was a problem between Jack and me."

Zach gave me a disbelieving yet flat look and I sighed heavily, giving in. Zach could be even more stubborn than I was and I absolutely refused to stay at his house until I revealed what was bothering me because that would be something he would do.

"It's not that big a deal," I started quietly, my hands still stirring the tea with my eyes firmly fixed on it. "Ever since the news came out, he seems to be-" I paused, trying to search for the right word to describe the current situation.

"Distancing himself from me."

Zach raised an eyebrow quizzically, "How? Please elaborate further."

I shot him a dirty look before continuing, "It's as if he's getting ready to leave. Like there's an invisible wall between us and I could feel us moving further and further away."

"Why do you think this is happening?" Zach pressed, his eyes deep in thought and I shrugged carelessly while staring into my cup of tea that had gone cold."I don't know and I'm not surprised. It's bound to happen sooner or later," I answered listlessly.

"What's that supposed to mean?"

"It means that no one would want to stick with me because I'm disabled!" I snapped, feeling angry tears well up in my eyes.

This was why I hated talking about my feelings. It always ended up with me in tears and I hated crying even though it was in front of Zach.

"What kind of rubbish are you spouting now? You're not disabled!" Zach scorned, his eyes glaring at me. I could see the anger in them due to the way I saw myself.

"I can't give him a family and he's the type to want one. At first, he took it well but now? Second thoughts are obviously creeping in! Why would he want someone like me?" I argued hotly, the possible reality of Jack actually leaving was setting in.

"Is that really how you value yourself? I get that it is a sore point but the guy obviously worships the ground you walk on, you must have misinterpreted the whole situation!" Zach retorted, his eyes flashing.

I pressed my lips into a thin line and turned my head away to avoid looking at him while blinking back the tears. Seeing how upset I was getting, Zach softened the glare on his and his tone gentled, "Look Em, go and talk to him about it. Assuming and guessing won't get you anywhere and if he really is upset about it, he's not worth your tears."

Swallowing harshly, I looked down at my lap, hoping that Zach wouldn't see the tear that managed to escape my eye and roll down my cheek.

"Now I think it is best to ask him and then talk to him. There isn't any point worrying and guessing and trying to figure out what's going on his mind," he said softly and eventually, I nodded glumly.

* * *

Jack Donnahue's POV

"You're being ridiculous," one of my many sister-in-laws commented as she perched herself onto the seat opposite me.

"Bugger off," I grumbled before scrolling through my phone, trying to ignore her and her very perceptive gaze.

I could feel her trying to pull the truth out of me with her eyes and I tensed, hoping that I wouldn't be able to portray anything. I was an actor, wasn't I? I could surely act as if nothing was wrong. However, the trouble was that my heart wasn't in it.

For the first time, I wished I was ordinary. I wished that i was someone who had a job in an office that worked from nine in the morning to five in the evening before heading home to have dinner and sleep before having the same whole routine the next day. I would be someone that wouldn't have reporters stalking my every move. I would be totally anonymous and I wouldn't have the constant worry that Emma would just leave.

"Jack," she warned and I glanced up to see her crossing her arms over her protruding belly that seemed about to pop any day from now. "Go away."

"Are you brooding about Emma?" She pressed and I shot her withering glare. "Why do you care?" I demanded to which Isadora casts her eyes down to her lap.

It was obviously clear that I was not over the previous incident where Isadora got all rude with Emma. And it was also very clear to Isadora that she was still not in my good books even though she had apologised and that both Emma and her were now on good terms.

"I see," she replied quietly before getting to her feet, "Well I'm sure whatever is happening, a good talk will solve it." With that, she walked off and again, I wondered how the hell my family could even enter my own house without a key.

It was about five minutes later that I realised I was due for dinner at Emma's where she would be cooking and I wondered if this was like a farewell dinner where she would be leaving?

At that very thought, my heart seemed to ache painfully and it felt like I was losing my breath. She couldn't leave, not when I was in love with her.

Throughout the drive to Emma's I could feel my gut clenching painfully for the very fear that she would break things off.

"Hey," Emma greeted with a small smile as I stepped into her house with my sunglasses and cap on. She leant upwards to press a chaste kiss on my cheek before stepping back. "Dinner would be grilled steak and potatoes if that's okay with you?" She chewed on her lips hesitantly and I nodded, brandishing her with my bottle of wine.

"That sounds good. I brought wine," I announced and immediately felt stupid. Obviously, she could see that I brought wine. I was being such an idiot.

"That's great," Emma replied before making her way back into the kitchen and I followed her absentmindedly. "Where's Ella?" I questioned, expecting to see the little blonde running out of the room in excitement.

Emma gave me a quick glance, "It's a father and daughter bonding day. Theo brought Ella to the zoo if I'm not wrong." She gestured towards the fridge and I got the hint and placed the wine in. "Dinner would be ready in ten minutes if that's okay with you?"

I offered her a wide smile, "Of course. Hey, you're cooking. I can't even toast bread."

Emma shot me a funny look which was a mix of disbelief and amusement before she turned to the oven while shaking her head as a wry smile accompanied her. "Of course. Here," she passed two sets of cutlery towards me. "You can set the table."

Doing so, it wasn't long before the food was ready and I was seated opposite her and we were digging into her food. Just looking at her made all the feelings I had for her rush to the surface.

I loved Emma.

I loved her for the way she could forgive easily. I loved her for the way she hated sprinkles and romance movies but tolerated it for me. I loved her for having witty remarks that made me laugh. I loved her for the way she could smile and my day was made. I loved everything about her.

However, how was I going to tell her that? I couldn't blurt it out like some idiot with his first crush. There was a fifty percent chance that she may leave and if I told her how I truly felt, I would be a humiliated fool.

"Jack, I think we should...talk," Emma started hesitantly, her eyes meeting mine anxiously and already, I could feel my heart speed up at the sombre tone she was using.

This was it. She was leaving, wasn't she? I could barely speak hence, I merely gave a short nod in return. What could I even say? Even though I was faced with the slight possibility that this could be happening, I didn't want to deal with it.

"I know that lately, we've been distant and-"

If it was possible, my heart would be out of my body as it was beating so fast and I felt like throwing up. Good God, I was pathetic.

"-I think its because of what we discussed a few weeks ago. Jack, please be honest with me. It's okay if you want to leave because I have a disability."

Wait what? What the hell was she spouting about? Disability? As far as I knew, Emma didn't have any- oh wait. She couldn't be talking about that, could she? Did she think that I would up and leave because she couldn't have children? Hadn't we discussed this before?

I furrowed my brows and leant in, "What?"

Emma remained silent as she stared at me evenly. "Hadn't we talked about this before? I'm not going anywhere because of that. I meant it last time and I still mean it now. Nothing can make me leave," I said earnestly, trying to convey how serious I was through my expression and my tone.

"Well, why were you so distant then?" Emma demanded shortly, her face not betraying a single emotion and I quite envied her for her impeccable poker face.

I shifted my jaw and met her gave evenly, "Because you said you were wanted to leave."

She blinked before narrowing her eyes, "I said no such thing."

"You did," I retorted. "Back when the press were giving crazy accusations. You said you wished you could just pack up and head off to another state. You leaving means leaving me."

Emma wrinkled her nose as she tried to recall whatever I was saying and I watched her silently. I hated that I sounded so needy and desperate through that little speech I gave. Fuck, was I an actor or not?

Suddenly, her eyes widened in recognition and she chewed her lower lip, her eyes were filled with guilt and regret. "Oh Jack, I didn't mean it. I mean, sure it was just a simple wish but I could never. I have my job and Ella and Theo and even you! Not to mention Zach."

Stubborn, I remained silent and fixed my gaze on my plate.

"It was just words. I didn't mean it. I was just so upset and frustrated with those horrid lies the press was spewing. I'm not leaving. I can't," she explained quietly, using a tone that was so serious that I couldn't help but notice.

I looked up and her hazel eyes were pleading with me to see her point of view even though her face was its usual passive expression. "I understand," I replied, a small smile forming on my face and Emma nodded, relieved.

"Good. I won't leave Jack unless you want me to." She reached over and gripped my hand gently as if she was trying to reassure me and I was thankful for that.

I was bloody in love with her and I wouldn't even know what to do with myself if she did leave.

The best part? I didn't even know when and how to tell her. Emma seemed like the sort to freak out if I confessed that. I wasn't going to put myself out there especially when I wasn't a hundred percent sure she felt the same way.

The anxiousness in my gut didn't disappear.

* * *

A/N: Hello lovelies! See I'm updating regularly! Anyway, there will be one last chapter after this and then the epilogue so yeah! Please give me a vote and a comment and let me know what you think! :)

Chapter 26-The Gathering

Chapter 26 - The Gathering

Jack Donnahue's POV

Emma huffed. It wasn't the first time she was doing so and it certainly wasn't going to be the last.

I couldn't help but smirk to myself as she pursed her lips before crossing her arms over her chest, silently telling me through her actions how displeased she was.

A month has passed since Theo Heywood had awoken from his coma and some of his friends were throwing a welcome back party for him. And by friends, it referred to his friends from Hollywood.

Of course, Theo gave me the almost impossible task of getting Emma to go with him, seeing that I was dating her. The mere second after asking her,

Emma refused profusely but after some coaxing - and begging - she agreed only with the condition that I go with her.

It wasn't exactly hard to say yes considering I was invited as well. Not that she knew or anything.

"Come on, lighten up! You're doing this for Theo," I coaxed and Emma snorted and shot me a sideway glance. "Right, why don't you be there in my stead especially now that the both of you are thick as thieves."

An amused grin crossed my face at that. It was true. After getting through that awkward stage where Theo tried to be all intimidating as I was dating his sister, we became really good friends, much to Emma's annoyance.

"Yes, but Theo needs some familial support and you're his sister!"

Emma scoffed and turned away from me, clearly deciding that I wasn't worth talking to at the moment. The party was at a fellow actor's house and he promised that it was just a small gathering and it was pretty casual.

Emma took some relief from the dress code and wore a pretty pink skirt and a black blouse with some low heels. I, on the other hand, was dressed in a pair of jeans and a plain white shirt accompanied with a jacket over.

And as we got into my car, I couldn't help but notice that we looked pretty good together from the reflection in the windows. To my relief and amusement, Emma was still shorter than me despite her heels giving her a slight height advantage.

"You do realise that I wouldn't know anyone at the party right?" Emma spoke up as she tried to change my mind about going which I blatantly ignored. Again.

"Okay, how about this, we'll just go for an hour and then we'll leave?" I bargained and Emma eyed me, her eyes getting all squinty as she scrutinised me before agreeing. "Alright, fine. But don't blame me if I act like a cold bitch with a Louboutin shoved up my arse."

I snorted and flashed her a teasing grin. "It's okay, I'll get sympathy from people wondering why someone so amazing and funny like me is dating someone so utterly awful."

"Yeah, any more arrogance from you, and I am going home because I'm allergic to it." Emma shot back with her eyes narrowed but I could see them lighting up in amusement.

"Allergic? I think you mean adoration," I teased and Emma rolled her eyes as a small smile played at the corner of her mouth. "You wish," she said and adjusted the hem of her skirt.

"Yes, I do," I replied and Emma made a face and was about to open her mouth to retort with something witty but mean when I parked the car. "This is not a small gathering. There are about a hundred people here," she exclaimed and glared at me as if I was hosting the party.

"Come on, I already said we'll just stay for an hour or so. It's just to check if your brother is dealing well with the sudden crowd and stuff," I replied and Emma's eyes softened at the mention of Theo. Slumping her shoulders in defeat, she exited the car

"Fine, but promise me, nothing more than an hour." She stared at me earnestly and I nodded, "I promise, we can get a drink after the gathering."

She sighed heavily and trudged reluctantly towards the pathway leading up to the big house and I quickly caught up with her and wrapped an arm around her shoulders.

"I'll be by your side the entire time alright?" I reassured.

Emma nodded her head but didn't respond and somehow, it felt like I was talking about a whole different situation in the end. I meant it, I would be by her side as long as she wanted me there.

That realisation almost made me jerk abruptly. I knew I wanted to be with Emma for the long-term and I knew she felt the same way. But where did that leave us? I hadn't even managed to summon the courage I had to tell her how I felt.

Just the thought of putting myself out there made me feel physically ill that I almost threw up right there and then but I forced that reflex action down and together we entered the house. I was a hundred percent sure that Gwennie, Isadora and Danielle would tell me I was a coward but they had no idea what they were talking about.

Pushing my thoughts on this subject aside, I decided to ponder about it later. There was plenty of time to think about the possible actions and scenarios that could happen when I finally summoned up the courage to tell Emma how I truly felt about her.

As we stepped into the house, I moved my arm that was wrapped around her shoulders to her waist and pulled her closer to me. I could tell she was worried and I didn't blame her. If I was in her shoes, I would react the exact same way or maybe even worse.

At first, no one gave us a second glance but soon enough, there were curious stares being shot our way and I could feel Emma tense up beside me from the attention we were getting. Some of the guests gave various sorts of smiles in our direction but mainly, there were loads of whispers and sideway glances.

Peering down at Emma, I couldn't help but let a soft chuckle escape my mouth. True enough, she had a bored but yet cold expression on her face as her eyes surveyed the room with well-concealed interest.

Emma's bitch mode was definitely switched on.

Along with smiles and curious glances, I also noticed a few appreciative stares thrown towards my girlfriend and I subconsciously tightened my grip on her waist.

"Jack! There you are! It's been ages! And this must be Emmaline, right? Heywood's sister? That kinda makes you a Heywood as well doesn't it?" A fellow actor of mine approached us, his curious eyes landing on Emma for a tad longer than was acceptable - well, it was to me.

I forced a smile and shrugged, "Life has just been so busy. But it's great to see you too Kev. And yes, this is my girlfriend Emma."

The actor let out a low whistle and his eyes darted towards mine, "Not that bad a bird you got there Donnahue." Emma's eyes narrowed just the slightest bit and inwardly I was cringing. To Emma, the man greeted, "It is very nice to meet you, Emmaline, I'm Kevin Thompson. If you ever get sick of old Donnahue, give me a call."

I opened my mouth to interject because I was certainly not old. I was just thirty for fuck's sake. That wasn't old. Wait, was it? But before I could say anything, Emma stepped forward, a hard but yet saccharine sweet smile on her face.

"Well, it's fortunate that I do not have your number then," she answered politely though her words spewed venom. "Excuse us please." Emma inclined her head and tugged me away from the man.

"Is the hour up yet?" she demanded impatiently and I blinked at her before continuously turning backwards to sneak glances back at Kevin. "Someone please call the fire brigade, the man just got burrrrrnt," I crowed in smug delight.

"Jack!" Emma shot me a flat look and opened her mouth to comment when Theo called out, "Emmy! It's great to see you here!"

Both of us turned around to see Theo heading towards us, a bright grin on his face.

"See, he's fine. Can we go?" Emma questioned hastily, her eyes darting about the room as if she was a bunny and was surrounded by a pack of starving wolves.

Looking down at her, it was plain as day that she was uncomfortable as hell and I agreed. Truthfully, parties weren't really my scene, you had to put in so much effort to be nice and if you weren't, rumours would start following you everywhere. I would rather be somewhere quiet with a tad more privacy than this.

Oh god, I really was old. Shit.

Apparently, I was so deep in thought that I didn't realise that Theo had left and Emma was tapping her foot impatiently, hinting heavily for us to leave.

"Jack," she started and her brown eyes pleaded with mine. "Alright, alright. Let's go." Again, my hand slid down to the small of her back and she visibly relaxed. We began leaving quietly and I gave some nods to people I recognised and soon enough we were walking out of the house.

"There's a perfect coffee house nearby-" I cut myself off when I realised that Emma had stopped walking and was now standing in the middle of the pathway that led to the parking lots. "Em? What-"

"My parents are here," she interjected in a hard tone that showed the strong feelings of resentment that she had towards her parents.

I turned to the direction Emma was staring coldly at. and was met with the sight of Henry and Adeline Heywood.

* * *

Emmaline Heywood's POV

"Emmaline darling, I'm so glad to see you here," my mother crooned in her faux falsetto voice and I could feel myself tense up. It was about five months that I had last seen them and that was at the previous hospital that Theo had stayed in when he was still in a coma.

I was still greatly appalled - and furious - that they had the nerve to film their tv show while my brother was in a coma.

"Jack, that coffee house sounds great. Let's go," I called and I could feel him staring at me warily but my eyes were firmly fixed on my parents who were watching the exchange between Jack and me.

"So it is true! Emmaline, you didn't tell me you're together with Jack Donnahue of all people! I had to find out from the news!" My mother gasped dramatically, her wrinkle-free face stretching into a weird expression due to the many surgeries she had gone for over the years.

"Yes, we are together," I gritted my teeth and from my peripheral view, I could see a group of people watching the escalating debacle.

My mother crossed her jewellery encrusted arms and stared me down, "I'm not surprised, you never tell me anything. You didn't even tell me I had a granddaughter!"

I shoved my purse to Jack who almost tripped trying to catch it before it fell to the ground but I couldn't bring myself to care. I was on the verge of reaching out to strangle her but I resisted with God given strength. "Why the hell should I be telling you anything? You disowned me!"

This time my father spoke up, his eyes narrowing on me, "You deserved it! You were being an ungrateful brat!"

This caught Jack's attention as his head snapped towards my parents. I could literally feel my blood boiling but the worst part was, I seemed to have lost the ability to speak. I was just so angry that the lump in my throat refused to go away. Worst of all, I could feel the threat of angry tears stinging in the back of my eyes.

Seeing that I wasn't shouting or even screaming at them, my parents took advantage of my silence and began shooting their horrid and hateful words at me. "Nothing to say?" my mother mocked, a cruel smile on her face as she surveyed me.

My eyes darted from the camera man that belonged to their stupid reality show filming everything and I was still tongue-tied.

"After everything we did for you, the acting classes, those modelling agents, what did we get in return? We certainly didn't get our money back? Your modelling career was gone the minute you got those scars and worst of all, you made us lose so much money after that accident!"

I could feel myself shaking. Shaking from rage and all the emotions were bubbling so close to the surface that I wanted to wring my parents' neck.

"Worst of all, you made your brother and his daughter - our granddaughter not part of our lives! You're not even worth to be part of the Heywood name!" my mother exclaimed, her voice shrill as she started to shriek.

By now, my hands had curled into fists and I'm pretty sure my nails were cutting into my palms from how hard I was clenching them. I was so close to losing it that I could barely breathe.

"What have we done to deserve an ungrateful child like you?"

That. Was. It.

However, before I could do anything, Jack stepped in, a cold thunderous expression formed on his features. Never had I seen him so upset or angry. This was even worse than the Isadora debacle. "You have no idea what the hell you are talking about," he said quietly, his arm reaching towards mine and he interlaced our fingers together.

Taken aback, my mother stared shrewdly at Jack. Using a disbelieving tone, she set her eyes on him as if he was an alien. "Excuse me?"

Jack straightened up. "Your daughter is one of the most amazing people I've ever met. And the both of you certainly had nothing to do with raising her," he paused and turned towards me. His eyes softened and he reached out to brush away a tear I hadn't realised had escaped.

I could feel my eyes welling up in more tears from the way he stared at me - like I was the most beautiful person alive. Like he cherished me with all of his heart. I've never been looked at that way before.

Jack turned his attention back to my parents and his features hardened into something more menacing. "From what I know and have seen, the both of you are horrid examples of how parents should be. I don't blame Emma for leaving everything she had behind nor for the fact that she never allowed Ella to meet the both of you."

"The both of you are only selfish, concerned about money and fame and you don't even care about the well-being of your own children. It's a damn shame that the both of you would treat your own flesh and blood - the woman I love this terribly!"

I blinked, unsure if I heard that right.

Wait what?

Did Jack just say what I thought he said? He couldn't have, could he? My heart was racing and my hands felt clammy but anxiousness was creeping in. He couldn't really feel that way could he?

"Why, I never-" my mother's indignant voice sounded but I cut her off.

"SHUT UP! Just fucking shut up!" I shouted, relieved that I was finally able to voice out my thoughts. Turning away from them, I quickly faced Jack who was staring at me with pure adoration on his face.

"I love you, Emma," he confessed softly and I could feel the heat of his gaze. It was so intense that I felt unusually warm. I could see that his hands were clenched so tightly as if he was feeling insecure or nervous on how I would respond.

Without thinking, I took a step closer towards him, my eyes searching his and I reached out and cradled the sides of his face before leaning in.

I didn't care about my parents or the fact that they were watching us. Neither did I care about the scene that they and Jack made. I didn't even care about the crowd or the cameras. I also didn't care about the possible headlines that would be splashed in the papers tomorrow. I couldn't even bring myself to care anymore.

I was in love with this man and nothing could ruin the moment or change my feelings for him.

I stepped closer to him and brushed my lips against his while murmuring against them, "I love you too."

At my confession, I could feel his hands encircle my waist along with the wide smile on his face. I could also feel his shoulders sag with relief and I pulled back slightly to see elation forming on his handsome features.

"Of course, I'm Jack Donnahue."

I couldn't help but snort in a very unladylike fashion before bursting into quiet laughter and then, I tugged him closer to me and our lips met.

-FIN-

* * *

A/N: Hey all! YES! This is the last chapter and there will be an epilogue posted sometime this week! Make sure you guys catch it! I hope you guys enjoyed this little story of mine because I did and it was a little different than my usual sort. I hope you guys enjoyed it and I love you all so much for supporting and being patient with me on this journey of Jack & Emma. Let me know your thoughts and whatnot and hopefully, I'll see you in my upcoming books/projects! <3

Also thank you to for the lovely cover below. Thanks so much dearie! <3

Epilogue

Epilogue

Emmaline Donnahue's POV

"And do you, take this woman to be your lawfully wedded wife?" The vicar asked as he turned to the groom who was beaming widely.

"I do."

The vicar continued turning to his right, "And do you, take this man to be your lawfully wedded husband?"

I narrowed my eyes and scowled irritatedly. "Is there a point to this?" I demanded.

Jack glared at me and crossed his arms over his chest defensively, "Of course there is!" He let out an exasperated huff and paused the movie that was playing on the screen and focused his full attention on me.

"Well, what exactly is the point?" I question, my eyes narrowing at his slouched posture.

"Are you serious? You don't even know?" Jack's eyes widened in what looked like a mix of horror and disbelief.

"Donnahue!" I snapped, losing my patience.

Jack turned to me, the horrified expression gone and was now replaced with a cheeky grin on his face. "Who are you calling? Me or yourself? Because we share the same name ever since you married me."

My lips twitched at that. No matter how hard I was trying to not show my amusement at his quips, I failed. Letting out a short laugh, I forced myself to become serious again."There is no way I'm watching this after the previous one," I complained while gesturing towards the screen where the rom-com just started.

It was a lovely Saturday evening and I was cooped up watching rom-coms after rom-coms because Jack thought we should be fully prepared. Never mind the fact that almost all movies are unrealistic and ridiculous, he had insisted and forced me to watch them.

Jack feigned a pout, "Please! We have to be prepared for our own wedding ceremony!"

"We are already married, I don't see why we have to go through with another ceremony," I pointed out, still not keen with the fact that everyone had insisted on us having an actual wedding ceremony, unlike the one that Jack and I had when we eloped two months ago.

"Em please! I don't want Gwennie ruining everything if she finds out that we don't even know how to plan a wedding!"

I rested my weight on my palms and stared up at him. "Shouldn't you know, considering you've acted in those silly movies and had to act in wedding scenes?" I questioned and Jack crossed his arms.

"I know! But this is different!" He stressed.

"How so?"

"Because it's our wedding!" he exclaimed exasperatedly as if he had repeated it countless times which was true. I had been hearing this ever since his family and Theo and Zach had found out we had eloped.

They were not angry that we had not told them that we were eloping, it was more of a shock and a surprise. Immediately, mere seconds after finding out from spotting both an engagement and a wedding band on my finger, the women had insisted on an actual wedding ceremony.

"And again, we are already married. I don't see the point," I repeated and Jack snorted. "Well, it's mostly to placate our family members rather than ourselves don't you think?" I asked and Jack sighed, "Yes, I know."

"Also, isn't it because we're trying to avoid the paparazzi? Having an actual wedding defeats the purpose of eloping isn't it?"

"Yes, Emma, I know-"

"Or are you insisting on having it because you're trying to hide the fact that you've continued in your family's disaster of proposing?" I interjected before allowing a smirk to form on my face.

Jack cringed and shuddered in mock agony as a red hint formed on his cheeks. "God, let's not speak about it again. It was even worse than Cameron's and Strider's proposals put together," he groaned in mortification as he slumped down onto the couch and stuffed a cushion over his face.

Immediately, a wide smile stretched across my face as that particular memory came about. It was something that I would never forget for the rest of my life.

* * *

2 months ago

"The food is lovely," I commented and spooned the chocolate dessert into my mouth. "The dessert is even better," I groaned in delight and Jack offered me a weak smile.

"That's great to see! I mean-uh that you like the dessert!" he grinned and fidgeted once more. "What's up with you?" I questioned, mildly curious as to why Jack was acting all out of sorts today and the last week.

Not that he wasn't unusually odd at times, but today, he was even more so.

"Nothing!" He hastily said and drummed his fingers anxiously.

"You're being...odd today," I observed and Jack forced a laugh that was so strained that if the atmosphere was any more awkward, I could cut it with a knife.

"Me? Odd? Hardly!" Jack flashed me a bright grin and shifted in his seat again.

I shrugged and turned away, reaching for my purse. "Alright, if we're done, maybe we could go?"

"NO!" Jack almost shouted and quickly lowered his volume down and looked around the restaurant warily. At my scandalised expression, he forced out a laugh, "I mean, no, we haven't had the wine yet."

By now, I was getting a little suspicious and I scrutinised him further. Apparently, studying Jack while he was nervous was not a good idea as he became even worse.

"Okay then," I said slowly and Jack exhaled deeply and waved his hand to catch the attention of the waiter and soon enough, two glasses of red wine were delivered to our table.

I was scrolling through my phone while occasionally sipping from the glass of wine, which I had to admit was really good when Jack cleared his throat.

"Em?"

Hearing my name, I looked up in question. "Yes?"

"Ah, well. I have something to say and hopefully-"

He began fumbling around in his jacket pocket while trying to maintain the conversation. "Uh, hopefully, you'll be able to listen and well, that's the reason I've brought you out today and-goddamnit where the fuck is it?"

I leant back into my chair and watched him in amusement as he began muttering under his breath while digging through his pocket.

"Anyway, I wanted to say- NO! I mean I wanted to ask-OH HOLY FUCK!"

My eyes widened in horror when Jack's elbow knocked over the candle on our table and a fire started on the table cloth.

"Oh my god Jack!" I hissed in panic and reached out to grab my glass of water to put the flames out when Jack beat me to it.

However, he used his wine glass instead and the flames grew bigger. "OH MY GOD!" He was almost shouting and I ignored him and attempted to douse the flames. Thankfully, it worked and the pristine white table cloth had a rather large burnt mark on it.

"Jack Donnahue," I mumbled, still in shock. Said man was panting from exertion and panic and began fanning himself with his hand and conveniently, his hand hit a waiter who had a tray full of dishes.

And as expected, everything came crashing down to the ground. The sound of plates breaking and people gasping and cursing sounded across the restaurant and I met Jack's frozen stare.

"I think it's best if we leave now," I offered quietly, my eyes wide and Jack nodded mutely with a stunned expression on his face as if he couldn't believe what he had just done.Thirty minutes later, we were strolling around a park in silence but, it was a comfortable one. I figured that Jack was still in shock that he set the table on fire and made it worse before knocking a couple of dishes onto the ground.

Clearly, Jack must not have passed Chemistry seeing that he splashed a drink containing alcohol over a rapidly growing flame.

"Emma," he began and we paused in the middle of the walkway.

"I've known you for more than a year and we've been together for about a year and I love you," he declared and a smile formed on my face. My earlier suspicions were right.

"I know you feel the same way, why else would you put up with me?" An awkward laugh came from his mouth and he continued, his hand taking mine while his eyes were locked on me. "So, would you do me the honour of marrying me?"

I began nodding, lost for words, despite knowing that he had been intending to propose the entire dinner ever since he showed how nervous he was.

"Really?" he breathed out as he stares at me reverently as if I had agreed to give him the stars and the moon.

I nod my head, a bright smile sneaking onto my face. "Yes, I'll marry you," I replied and a brilliant smile formed on his face and he tugged me closer and his arms snaked around my waist.

"Wait," I started and stared at him expectantly while pulling away slightly from his embrace.

"What?" he asked, his brows raised and I shifted my weight on my feet. "Where is it?"

"Where is what?" He asks, utterly confused and I gave him a flat look. "The ring?" I wave my hand in front of his face and Jack brightened.

"Right! It's here-" Jack flashed me a beam and dug his right hand into his pocket and frowned before yanking harshly. "It's just here but, its stuck!" He growled in frustration and I eyed his movements warily."Yes, I got it!" he cried out in triumph but unfortunately, his elbow - the very same one that had hit the waiter - knocked into me as he yanked the ring out of his pocket and I lost my balance before tumbling into the lake.

"OH SHIT!"

"JACK!"

* * *

At first, I was no doubt upset but I managed to see the funny side after I had my shower and clean clothes on.

"I really wish you wouldn't bring that up, it's mortifying," he moaned into the cushion and began repeatedly smashing his face with it.

"But it's unique," I offered helpfully and leant back onto the couch. "Who else could say that the night they got engaged, their fiancé set fire to a table, made a huge scene at a restaurant and knocked his fiancée into a lake while proposing?"

Jack groaned once more, "Stop, please. Just. Stop."

I let out a laugh and rested my feet horizontally onto his lap. "Well, it is an important memory. One that I will always cherish," I said teasingly and Jack shoved the cushion away from his face.

"How about I propose to you again, properly and we'll forget about the most embarrassing incident of my life?" He asked hopefully.

"No," I said and grinned at him. "I think it was cute. You being all nervous and stuff until you messed everything up."

Jack scowled and pushed my legs off his lap. "That's easy for you to say," he scoffed and turned away from me.

I sighed and slumped back onto the sofa, giving in. "So I'm just telling you that I wouldn't be inviting my parents to our wedding."

My husband - God, that's weird, I mused - turned towards my direction and scrutinised me. "Really?"

"Really," I confirmed lightly, not choosing to look at him because I knew that Jack would definitely take it as a way of me apologising for my teasing.

Jack shrugged and gave me a lopsided grin. "Well, you're known to make right decisions. You married me," he supplied with a cheeky smirk as he wiggled his eyebrows at me.

I rolled her eyes and scoffed, a hint of a smile on my lips as I recognised the opportunity to get a shot in. "Really? I thought that decision was to prove that I should be in a mental institution," I retorted to which Jack scowled.

"Funny," he grumbled under his breath and I laughed.

Jack shot me a dry glance as he pressed the play button for the movie to continue playing. And together we sat there, watching. His arm was wrapped around my shoulders and my head was resting on his chest with my body curled onto his.

Right there and then, I really knew what happiness truly felt like.

* * *

A/N: OH MY GOODNESS! This is literally the end of Into The Spotlight! I hope you guys enjoyed it and please vote and comment to let me know what you think/felt while reading this little idea of mine that popped into my head while watching Leo get his first Oscars. Yes, I know. I'm weird.

Anyway, I've got a new story lined up (gonna do some shameless plugging) It's called Burning Castles and here's a synopsis so please go to the book to read info and comment to let me know what you guys think. Pretty please?

Synopsis:

In a world where the wealthy rule and the poor are enslaved and mistreated, orphan Adrastea Bones is barely surviving until she is needed for her skills as a healer.

Brought before Rhydderch Thomas, the leader of a resistance to revolutionise the current world they are living in, Adrastea realises that they are soulmates due to the words marked on their skin.

In the end, the only thing Adrastea knows is that there's a price to pay for power.